about the author

chad kultgen is also the author of *The Average American Male, The Lie,* and *Men, Women & Children*. He is a graduate of the USC School of Cinematic Arts and lives in California.

D0036720

the average american marriage

also by chad kultgen

The Average American Male
The Lie
Men, Women & Children

the **average** american **marriage**

a novel

chad kultgen

HARPER ⬤ PERENNIAL

NEW YORK • LONDON • TORONTO • SYDNEY • NEW DELHI • AUCKLAND

HARPER ● PERENNIAL

THE AVERAGE AMERICAN MARRIAGE. Copyright © 2013 by Chad Kultgen. All rights reserved. Printed in the United States of America. No part of this book may be used or reproduced in any manner whatsoever without written permission except in the case of brief quotations embodied in critical articles and reviews. For information address HarperCollins Publishers, 10 East 53rd Street, New York, NY 10022.

HarperCollins books may be purchased for educational, business, or sales promotional use. For information please write: Special Markets Department, HarperCollins Publishers, 10 East 53rd Street, New York, NY 10022.

FIRST EDITION

Library of Congress Cataloging-in-Publication Data is available upon request.

ISBN 978-0-06-211955-1

13 14 15 16 17 OV/RRD 10 9 8 7 6 5 4 3 2 1

Christmas with the Wife and Kids

Same old bullshit.

Happy Fucking Birthday to Me

We drop the kids off at Alyna's friend Isabelle's house. I stare at Isabelle's tits as Alyna tells her what time the kids should be in bed and what type of shit they should eat for dinner. I stare at her ass as Alyna hands over the giant bag of shit we constantly carry around with us, which contains various bottles, asswipes, books, DVDs, toys, etc. Isabelle is not hot. She has a dumpy ass, sloppy tits, big gums, and a forehead that's noticeably too small for a human face. I want to fuck the shit out of her. I know the only reason I want to fuck the shit out of her is that she is not Alyna. Knowing this doesn't make the desire any less tangible, doesn't make me wonder what her pussy tastes like any less. I imagine several babysitting scenarios in which the kids are asleep and I fuck Isabelle in various positions, locations, and holes.

We kiss and hug the kids and then we each give Isabelle a hug before we leave. At the end of my hug I purposely brush her ass with my right hand. It's too brief to give me any concrete information about the make of her ass, but I imagine it must be disgusting naked. I still want to fuck her.

Alyna drives, because wherever she's taking me for dinner is supposed to be a surprise. She says, "So, you really have no idea where we're going?"

"Nope."

"Good. I think you'll like it."

"We can just go home and order in if you want. A night without the kids is the best present you could give me."

"Don't be a dick."

"I'm not. It's just been a while since we've had a night to ourselves. I actually can't even remember the last one." This is a lie. The memory of the last night we spent alone feels like it was burned into my fucking brain with a soldering iron. Alyna's parents were in town staying in a hotel and they wanted to spend the night with the kids so we left them in the hotel. It was the last time Alyna and I fucked—at least two months ago.

She says, "Well, I want to take you out to dinner and then we'll have all night together."

We drive from Woodland Hills over the hill into LA proper and pull up in front of Jar. I fucking hate Jar. Alyna loves it. We've eaten here a dozen or so times, always at her request. I told Alyna that I liked one of the imported beers they have once. To Alyna, this means I like the restaurant. She says, "You excited for some St. Peter's Cream Stout?"

I say, "Yeah."

Although she's gotten better about it, Alyna dominates ninety percent of the conversation by asking how I think the kids are doing with her friend Isabelle. She brings up things like the fact that they've never stayed with her before, things like it's a weekend so Andy, at least, will be used to staying up a little later, things like wondering if she remembered to put Jane's Pocahontas doll in the bag of shit we left with Isabelle. She misses the kids already.

Strangely, I do, too, but only a little. Not enough to keep me from almost jerking off under the table at the promise of the fucking that's going to follow the shitty meal I choke down at Jar. I drink five St. Peter's Cream Stouts during the dinner, which is enough to get me pretty drunk, already planning to attempt anal sex, knowing that I can use my inebriation as an excuse for the attempt if my birthday isn't enough to make Alyna receptive to the idea from the start.

Alyna pays the bill with our joint credit card and says, "So, how'd you like your birthday dinner?"

I say, "It was great. Thank you. Now let's get out of here."

"Aren't we an eager beaver? You know there's a second part to your birthday present tonight."

"What's the second part?"

"You'll have to wait until we get home."

Once we're home, I take off my clothes and get in bed. She tells me to wait, that she has to get the second part of my present, and I'm already guessing that it's some lingerie I couldn't care less about. She comes into the bedroom and I'm right. She's wearing a black lace bra and panties that I'm sure she bought with the joint credit card, too. She says, "You like?"

I don't give a shit. I say, "Yeah. You're hot. Now take it off and get over here."

She says, "Not yet, just watch. I worked on this."

She proceeds to do an uncoordinated strip routine around the room. It's a bizarro version of some of the worst strippers I can remember seeing in places like Reseda and Torrance. I can almost appreciate the effort, but it's completely unnecessary, a waste of what might be the only time we'll have without the kids for the foreseeable future. I get up out of bed and cut her routine short by pulling her panties off and undoing her bra so she's completely naked. I drag her back down onto the bed and kiss her. It's been so long since anyone but me has touched my cock that when I feel her hand start to go down my stomach I instantaneously get a hard-on that could drill a hole in concrete.

She starts sucking my dick. I try to remember the last blowjob I got from her and I can't. I reach down and grab one of her legs, pulling on it, giving her the hint that I want to sixty-nine. She says, "Just let me do you."

I say, "It's my birthday and I want your pussy in my face."

"Okay, okay, calm down."

With the birthday obligation initiated she has no choice but to straddle my face while she sucks my dick. As she brings one of her legs across my face and settles her cunt back toward my mouth, I overlook the patch of leg hair on her ankle where she missed the last time she shaved to notice two more-important things that I've been completely unaware of for the entirety of the past year because we haven't sixty-nined or fucked in any position that would yield this specific view. Number one: The backs of her legs are covered in cellulite. Her ass has gotten much larger since we got married. There's no denying that. I find that I don't really mind it. I even kind of like it. Even though it's big, it has a nice shape. But the shape looks like it's been sitting on hot gravel for the past year. The cellulite is not easy to ignore. But since I have no fucking choice, I do my best to ignore it by moving my eyes to her pussy. And that's when I notice Number two: The inch or so of skin between Alyna's pussy and asshole, which used to be smooth and perfect, is mangled by what looks like a scarred-over hacksaw wound.

There's only a split second in which I am completely confused by it, completely in the dark as to what could have caused it and how I never noticed it before. Then I remember: She had to have an episiotomy when she had our youngest kid, Jane. As I lick at her clitoris I think about the fact that we haven't done the sixty-nine since Jane was born, a little over a year ago. I think about the fact that Alyna used to have a perfect pussy and a perfect asshole and a perfect inch-long piece of cute pink skin in between them that always smelled like cinnamon and peaches. These things, as superficial as they may seem, attracted me to her originally. I think about the fact that she'll never be the same. She'll never be the girl I saw for the first time on that airplane. The view of her asshole and her pussy in this position will never be as good as it was. I wonder if she knows about the scar. I don't know what my taint looks like. She probably doesn't either.

I lick at the scar a little bit just to see what it feels like on my tongue. I try to remember what her pussy felt like in my mouth before the scar. I can't.

After a few minutes of sixty-nining, Alyna says, "I bet you want some reverse cowgirl, don't you?" She knows it's my favorite position.

I can't handle looking at the episiotomy scar anymore, which is unfortunate because all of my favorite sexual positions would give me a direct view of it. Suddenly, my preplanned attempt at anal sex is now just conjuring up irrational images in my mind of Alyna's episiotomy scar being split open by my dick. So on the one night that I'm granted sexual carte blanche, I realize I'll have to settle for something far more mundane than I would have normally. Even more depressing to me is the fact that I haven't fucked in so long that fucking missionary, or having Alyna ride my dick, will probably make me blow a load just as quickly as any other position would have, even if her pussy wasn't hideously disfigured.

I say, "No, just get on top."

She reaches over to the nightstand and gets out a rubber, which she claims to hate using in our increasingly infrequent sexual encounters but also makes no effort to remedy by going back on the pill. She says she wants to try to lose weight now that we're done having kids and the pill makes it difficult.

She does me the courtesy of ripping the wrapper open but hands me the rubber to put on myself. This exact interaction before fucking has become too routine for her to even think about putting the rubber on my dick herself, even on my birthday.

Once I put the rubber on, and she checks to make sure it's rolled down my cock far enough and securely fitted, she rides me for what I estimate to be about ten minutes before saying, "Just finish."

"What about you?"

"I don't know if I can tonight."

"Why not?"

"I just don't think I can. I'm thinking about the kids."

"Do you want me to go down on you or something? What can I do? I want you to cum, too."

"It's just one of those nights. I don't think I can. You should just finish."

I can't remember the last time I made Alyna cum. Since we had our first kid, Andy, the frequency of our sexual encounters fell off the charts, but so did her interest in them, and so did her ability to achieve orgasm as easily as she used to. I was hoping that on my birthday she could muster enough enthusiasm to enjoy herself while we fucked, and even if she couldn't cum maybe she'd at least fake it well enough that I could delude myself into thinking she was having a decent time. The more I think about it as I fuck her, the more I realize that the thing that bothers me the most about her not cumming has nothing to do with me feeling inadequate or feeling like less of a man or even a basic desire to give my wife pleasure. What's actually disappointing me is that she doesn't seem to care at all about the fact that she can't cum. The act of achieving an orgasm has somehow become so uninteresting or unimportant to her that she's not even willing to attempt it. I wonder why she fucks me at all and I can only come to the conclusion that it's just to placate me. This would explain the extremely low frequency with which we engage in any kind of sexual activity.

She says, "Come on. Cum for me."

I'm tempted to just stop fucking her, to watch some poker or *How It's Made* while she falls asleep and then sneak into the office to jerk off to some Riley Steele porn. Since I don't know when the next time I'll get to fuck might be, though, instead I grab her by the hips, squeeze into the fat around the upper part of her ass, and fuck her as hard as I can from underneath.

There isn't a glimmer of pleasure or ecstasy or anything even approaching sexual arousal in her eyes as she looks down at me, not even caring enough about any of it to hope it will be over soon. It's like she's waiting for the parking pay machine at the Beverly Center to spit her ticket back out after she's paid her two dollars. She says, "Yeah, fuck me until you cum," but she doesn't mean a word of it. I've never fucked a RealDoll, but I imagine it's something like this— except that a RealDoll would have a better body, a tighter pussy, and no episiotomy scar.

After a minute or so I close my eyes, try to remember one of the first times we fucked in my old apartment on a rare rainy day in West-wood, and reach up and grab one of her tits, which have both begun to sag significantly, probably as a result of her insistence on breast-feeding both of our kids. I squeeze it hard enough to make her say, "Ouch," and then I blow my load.

She gets off of me before my dick is even finished spitting out the last pump of cum, kisses me on the cheek, says, "Happy birthday," then rolls over and turns on the TV. I get up and go to the bathroom. I peel off the rubber and wrap it in a wad of toilet paper, mash it down as far as I can in the trash so my kids won't accidentally find it, then wonder how in the fuck this became my life.

He Smiles

I get off work at six. I get home at six forty-five. I eat dinner with Alyna and the kids at seven. Alyna gives the kids their baths at seven-thirty. So the thirty minutes from seven-thirty to 8 P.M. on every weeknight are mine. I can usually get in at least two games of *Modern Warfare*, sometimes three. I'm in the middle of my second game of Team Death-match on the Paris map and somebody on the opposite team just got Juggernaut when my son, Andy, comes out of the bathroom naked. I just catch him out of my peripheral vision, trying not to turn my full attention away from the game, when he says, "Look, Daddy, he smiles." He's four. He says fucked-up things that make no sense all the time. I stopped trying to figure out most of the shit he says a long time ago, but the phrase "Look, Daddy, he smiles" implies that my son wants me to look at something, and I'm curious who this "he" is. So I look away from the game and see my son standing by the hallway that leads back to the bathroom. He's completely naked, hair still wet from his bath, and he's holding his cock, looking down at it and laughing. But he's not just holding his cock. He has the head kind of turned sideways so the hole in his dick is horizontal instead of vertical, and he's pinching the head with the index finger and thumb on each of his hands, stretching the hole and twisting it up on the ends so it does, in fact, look like a tiny smile. I look away from his cock and back to my game as quickly as I can, wondering if I did shit like that when I was his age. Probably.

He says it again: "Look, Daddy, he smiles."

I say, "Yeah, I saw it."

He says, "No! Look longer."

I don't know what the fuck I'm supposed to do. I'm sure there is some way to respond to him, some proper, child-psychologist-approved manner in which I am supposed to interact with him at this point in his psychological development that won't leave any lasting negative effect, but all I can imagine is me saying the wrong thing and Andy ending up with a limp dick for the rest of his life or feeling like a woman trapped in a man's body or becoming a pedophile. I try to ignore him and hope he'll wander back into the bathroom, where I assume Alyna will know how to handle it. But he says it again, this time with more urgency: "Daddy, look! He smiles!" He really wants me to look at the little show he's putting on with his fucking cock, really give it the attention he feels it deserves. So I do it.

I look away from my game of *Modern Warfare* and stare right at my four-year-old son's dick as he twists it up as far as the skin will stretch. He starts bouncing up and down, doing a little dance, happy that I'm paying attention.

He says, "Can yours smile, daddy?"

Again, I have no idea what to say. I reason that I probably shouldn't make him feel isolated or strange or different from his dad in any way. So I say, "Yeah, mine can smile."

He says, "Make him smile. I want to see."

I imagine myself comparing smiling dicks with my son for a few seconds before Alyna comes out, sees him mangling his cock, and says, "Andy, you were supposed to put on your PJs."

He says, "Look, Mommy, he smiles."

Before I can even take note of how Alyna reacts, she says, "Yes, he does. But once it's nighttime he needs to sleep."

Andy says, "Okay, Mommy," drops his dick, and lets my wife hustle him off to bed. Even though she barely fucks me anymore, she's a good mom. That's the last thought I give the situation before getting in one more game of Free-for-All, in which I get demolished by a player I assume is a guy based on the gamertag 420BONERKING who goes 30-4. Then Alyna comes out of the kids' bedroom, turns off the Xbox, and says, "They're asleep. Game over. *American Idol*. Then bed. I'm exhausted."

This is the exact announcement Alyna makes every night, with only minor variation where the name of the reality-TV show is concerned. After she watches *American Idol*, she says, "I'm going to bed. You coming?"

I say, "Yeah, just need to check some work e-mails real quick," then I wait for her to go into the bedroom and I go to the office, where I turn the sound on the computer down as low as possible without turning it completely off, jerk off to some pregnant porn, blow my load in my hand, go to the guest bathroom, wash my hand, then go into the bedroom to find Alyna already asleep and snoring.

The last thought that crosses my mind before I enter dreamless sleep is a memory of fucking Casey, the girlfriend I had before Alyna, in a tiny hotel room with the window open on a trip we took to Catalina Island when we were young.

chapter three

Meeting with My Boss

For the last three hours I've been sitting at my desk drinking green tea because it's supposed to help me live longer and trying to write a proposal I know no one will ever read. I decide to reward myself with a long walk to the bathroom to take what I hope will be the longest piss of my life, followed by a liberal washing of my hands. I assume I can waste at least ten minutes on these two activities.

I open the door to the first-floor bathroom just in time to hear what sounds like somebody dumping a can of Dinty Moore beef stew onto wet concrete, followed by a long exhale. I look under the door of the only occupied shitter and don't recognize the shoes, so I have no idea who's responsible for my burning lungs as I walk to a urinal and unzip my pants, disappointed that my only minutes of respite from a job I hate have been ruined by the unknown guy opening a portal to the foulest pit of hell directly in his asshole.

Just as I'm starting to get jealous of whoever it is, because I assume they'll get to spend more of their work day in the bathroom than I will, I hear a flush. Then the door opens and my boss, Lonnie, steps out, still zipping his pants back up. He breaks one of the cardinal rules of bathroom etiquette and looks me directly in the eye through our reflections in the mirror. My cock is in my hand and I'm pissing as I feel obligated to recognize our shared glance in some way. I nod. He returns it.

My cock is still in my hand when he steamrolls the rest of the cardinal rules of bathroom etiquette and starts a full-on conversation with me. He turns the water on at the faucet closest to me and says, "Glad I caught you in here. Save me a trip to your office this afternoon," and puts his hands under the running water. No soap.

I'm trying to maintain some shred of composure in the situation so I don't say anything. I just nod again.

He says, "Know that intern, Jim or Stan or whatever?"

I nod.

He says, "Just told me he's leaving at the end of the week. Still have a mountain of old reports and proposals that need to be filed. Rather not pay someone to come in and do it, if you catch my drift. Mind rounding up another intern to replace him?"

I try to just shrug my shoulders as if to imply through body language that I'm responding with an attitude of compliance, but I can tell he won't get it. Instead I shrug my shoulders and say, "No problem," while my dick is still in my hand.

Lonnie says, "Great. Just call USC or UCLA or wherever we got this last one from. Or even CSUN or something. Guess it's closer. Probably the way to go. Thanks."

Then he does a shitty job of drying his hands with one paper towel and pats me on the shoulder. My cock is still in my hand and he still hasn't used any soap. I finish pissing, zip my pants back up, wash my hands with soap for much longer than necessary, dry them, and then go back to my desk. I stare at the proposal for a few seconds and then decide to take the long way around the first floor to the kitchen to slowly refill my green tea.

chapter four

Human Garbage

Alyna gives me shit when I call her and tell her that my buddy, Todd, wants to meet me after work for a few beers. She says, "You know I don't care if you want to get beers with Todd, but you have to give me more than three hours' notice."

I wonder why she'd require more notice. I know she has no plans that my impromptu after-work beers could possibly be ruining. I assume it's just some personal-consideration issue she thinks is at play, even though it's really not. I say, "He said he had something important to talk to me about. I'll be home before ten."

"Okay, but seriously, before ten. And you owe me a foot rub."

"Okay. See you at ten."

"You said before ten."

"I meant ten at the latest."

"At the latest."

"Yeah, that's what I said."

"Okay. Love you."

"Love you, too."

I hang up and catch myself literally shaking my head in disbelief at the shit I have to deal with in order to meet a friend for a few beers after work. I wonder if other married guys go through similar shit. I wonder if other married guys at least get to fuck their wives with some regularity. That would make the shit more tolerable, at least. I'm guessing they endure the exact same shit.

I close my spreadsheets, shut down my computer, lock the door to my office, and wonder how Gina, our receptionist, likes to be fucked as I tell her good night and head out to my car. As I drive to meet Todd, I decide it's doggy-style with a finger in her asshole.

Todd's already sitting at the bar in Firefly on Ventura when I walk in. He's on his second beer. He says, "What's yip, deuce?"

I say, "What?"

"I tried texting 'What's up, dude?' to you today and the swipe shit on my phone turned it into 'What's yip, deuce?' so I'm making that my new 'What's up, dude?' So what's yip, deuce?"

I sit down next to him and say, "Same old shit, man."

"How those kids treating you?"

"As well as kids can treat you, I guess. They cry, they shit their pants, they require constant attention."

"Sounds fun."

"It's not."

I order a beer and say, "So what's yip, deuce? What'd you want to tell me?"

"Dude, nice usage. Nikki wants to move in with me."

"And . . ."

"And I think I'm gonna cut her loose."

"Seriously? I thought you were into her. You guys have been together for a long time, right?"

"A year, dude. Longest girlfriend of all time. I was seriously into her. Her tits are great, she loves to fuck all the time, she usually smells pretty good, sometimes she cooks me shit, she's even pretty cool— knows about movies and TV shows and shit."

"Then what's the deal?"

"She's human garbage, dude. She's fucking twenty-eight. She waits tables and still thinks she's going to be a singer and a model and all of this other bullshit that everyone but her knows is a fucking pipe dream. I can't fucking listen to her tell me about how she's going to get a band together and start doing shows anymore."

"Sounds real bad."

"Fuck you. It is. She's just annoying as fuck with this singing shit, and now I guess because we've been going out for so long, she's comfortable enough to fart around me. And she pisses with the door open."

"So the romance is gone."

"Do you know how fucking fast morning wood goes away when you walk into the bathroom to piss because the fucking door's open and you see your girlfriend grunting while she's taking an actual shit? I don't think I can deal with it anymore, dude."

"That sucks, but you gotta do what you gotta do, I guess."

"I know, but then what the fuck do I do? I ain't getting any younger, dude. I doubt I can find another chick that I like even remotely as much as Nikki, and I'm pretty close to outright hating her."

"That doesn't sound good."

"It's not. It sucks dick."

"So why did you want me to come out? Are you asking my advice here or what?"

"No. I'm going to pull the plug. But I figure I should fuck her a few more times, cum in her ass, cum on her face once or twice—fuck, maybe even get some video of it. You know, really concentrate on getting some good memories to jerk off to once it's all over. And then in a few weeks she'll bring up the moving-in thing again and I'll say I don't want to and that'll probably be it. What I want to ask you is, can I count on you to step it up with going out and being a wingman?"

"Fuck, man, I have kids and shit. Alyna wasn't real happy about me even coming out to meet you tonight for a few beers."

"Thank you for validating my choice to dump Nikki with that

statement. I'm never going to get married. I can't fucking end up like you. I'll kill myself. No offense."

"It's all right."

"Don't you ever miss when we'd go out and get hammered and wrangle some random bitches?"

"Yeah, of course, but we're fucking old now, man. I miss it in the way a pro baseball player who's fifty probably misses the way he could hit a five-hundred-foot home run when he was twenty."

"Dude, no offense again, but you were never a pro baseball player of picking up chicks."

"Whatever, man. But right now we're the creepy old guys sitting at the end of the bar who we used to fucking make fun of when we were young. I'm not too into that."

"Really?" Todd indicates the other end of the bar with a head nod. I look in the direction he's nodding and see a guy who's definitely creepier and older than Todd and me. I say, "Fuck, man. That's some serious old and creepy. We're getting there, though."

"That's not how I see it at all. We're in a sweet spot, dude. Old skanks will fuck us because we're younger than they are but not too young to be able to pick up a check at Crustacean or some shit, and young skanks will fuck us because we have our shit together enough to even be able take them to a joint like Crustacean. Look at those two bitches." Todd nods toward two girls sitting on a couch in the corner. They look young, probably in their early twenties. He says, "Let's try to pick them up tonight."

I say, "No."

He says, "I'm not saying we fuck them or anything, just see if we can still do it."

I say, "Just to see if we can? There are only two outcomes and they're both bad. One, they fucking laugh at us and we confirm my suspicion that we're way too old to be doing shit like this. Or two, they're actually into us, which is even fucking worse because I can't fuck them, so instead I go home gritting my teeth so fucking hard at the thought of one of their tight asses on my dick that I give myself TMJ or some shit."

"Why can't you fuck one of them?"

"I'm fucking married, dickhead."

"We all make decisions. Now don't be a fucking pussy." Then he gets up off his bar stool and makes his way over to the two girls.

I stay where I am and watch him from across the room. He sits down next to one of the girls and starts talking. He talks to them for a minute or so, and neither of them seems receptive at first, but then he makes some kind of face, clearly telling a joke or some funny story, and he gets one of them to laugh. Then he points over to me and both of the girls look in my direction. Todd beckons me over with a wave of his hand and I find myself getting up from my seat. On the surface I know I'm doing this to help my friend, to not be a dick to him in his time of need. But below that, I can feel myself hoping that I can still pick up a chick, that I haven't become too old and too married to get one of these two girls to think of me as someone whose dick she wants in her pussy, that I have any small piece of the person I used to be somewhere still inside me, that I'm still alive.

I sit down next to them. Todd says, "This is Sandy and this is Kayla." I try my best to be amicable, to laugh when it seems appropriate, to be interesting and charming, and it seems like I'm making some headway. After maybe half an hour of talking to these girls, Sandy, a recent graduate of UCSB who came to Los Angeles to pursue a career in acting, touches my arm as she tells me the name of her cat is Valentine. It seems like she's flirting.

Todd, too, seems to be making headway with Kayla with exaggerated stories about his travels around the world as a reality-television producer. It slowly occurs to me that I would have no trouble finding girls to fuck if I were to find myself single again. Then Sandy says, "Is that a wedding ring?"

Before I can answer Todd says, "It was. His wife died almost two years ago, but he keeps the ring on to remember her." I shake my head at Todd, silently offering my disapproval at his lie but not wanting to blow it for him with these girls, who both immediately offer their condolences to me.

We drink and talk about nothing important with these two girls for a few hours, until I notice that it's almost ten. I want to stay. I want to see how far this could actually go. I wonder how pissed Alyna would be if I got home late. I could text her and tell her we're having a few more beers, but I know it wouldn't matter. She'd be pissed, with or without the text, if I didn't get home by ten. I say, "Well, ladies, it's been great meeting you. I have to be up early for work tomorrow, so I'm going to call it a night."

Todd offers his objections, and the girls follow suit, but I tell them I have a very important meeting early in the morning. The reality is that I have a wife, a living wife, who will not suck my dick for a period of time that is even longer than normal if I come home late.

I give Todd some cash for my drinks, say good-bye to Sandy and Kayla, get hugs from them both, hope Alyna won't smell their perfume on me, and head out to my car. I make it home a few minutes after ten, which Alyna is not happy about but is not genuinely pissed about, either. I rub her feet as promised to soothe any animosity she might have. I'm still a little buzzed when I get in bed, so I try to coax my wife into fucking me by rubbing my erection up against her ass when she rolls over. She ignores it and pretends to sleep.

I don't jerk off once she actually falls asleep. Instead I stare at the ceiling, happy. Knowing that a random chick I met in a bar would have fucked me, that if I had to I could still go into the wild and hunt for my dinner, calms me more than blowing a load into my hand ever could. I think that for a few minutes, then I start thinking about Sandy's tits and about what it would have been like if I had fucked her or gotten her to suck my dick. I slide out of bed, leaving Alyna sleeping, and go into the office.

I search for a clip of a girl getting fucked who looks as close to Sandy as I can find. I find one of a blond bitch with smallish tits, a big

ass, and shoulder-length hair that is similar to what I remember Sandy's looking like. I scroll through the video until I come to a segment
that has her riding the guy's cock in a POV shot. I jerk off for less than
a minute and blow my load all over my hand. I clear the computer's
browser history, go to the bathroom, wipe the semen off my hand with
one of the wipes Alyna uses to clean the kids' asses, sneak back into
bed undetected, and sleep peacefully.

An Average Sunday

9:20 A.M. Wake up with a hard-on.

9:21 A.M. Sneak into the bathroom while Alyna is downstairs with the kids and start jerking off over the toilet while imagining the receptionist from my office on her knees sucking my dick.

9:24 A.M. Hear someone coming up the stairs. Quickly sit down, bending my hard-on down under the seat and into the toilet. Pretend to be shitting when my son, Andy, wanders into the bathroom and shows me a picture he drew of our house.

9:25 A.M. Lose hard-on.

10:25 A.M. Hold Jane while Alyna clears the breakfast dishes and Andy runs around the living room screaming, "Moriarty is king! Moriarty is king!" Almost start to wonder what in the fuck he's talking about but I know that's a futile exercise so I just ignore him.

11:16 A.M. Try to watch some of the morning football game when

Alyna steps in front of the TV holding Jane up to my face and says, "Does it look like she has pinkeye or something?" I say, "No, she looks fine."

11:22 A.M.   Stifle anger as Alyna mutes the game so she can call the kids' pediatrician. From the pieces of the conversation I can overhear I figure out that Dr. Powell is making a special appointment for us on a Sunday, which means instead of watching the game I'll get to pay him a few hundred dollars to tell me that my kid does not have pinkeye.

12:36 P.M.   Watch Dr. Powell write a prescription for antibiotic eyedrops that are used to treat pinkeye.

12:50 P.M.   Hold Jane down as she screams and kicks while Alyna forces her eyelids open and administers the drops. Answer "No" to my son's question "Are you guys torturing her?"

1:04 P.M.   Strap the kids into their car seats. Hope the third child's birthday party that I'll be attending this month will have booze for the adults so I don't kill myself.

1:06 P.M.   Buckle my own seat belt and wish my son hadn't stopped me from jerking off.

2:18 P.M.   Pound my fourth Winnie the Pooh paper cup full of chardonnay. Ignore the disapproving looks from the other parents at this shitty kid's birthday party. See a hot younger mom bending over to tie her tub-of-shit kid's shoe. Think about fucking her in the ass. Wonder if she fucks her husband more than Alyna fucks me.

2:33 P.M.   Take a shit at the kid's birthday party. Hope Jane gives at least one of these kids pinkeye. Conjure an elaborate scenario in which Jane does give the hot younger mom's kid pinkeye, forcing us to meet randomly while filling eyedrop prescriptions at Walgreen's, which leads to her sucking my dick in the backseat of her car, which I imagine to be the Volvo station wagon I saw parked out front. Wonder if I can jerk off in a minute or under. Wipe my ass. Get out my phone. Cue up the first clip I come to on NudeVista.com, which is a girl getting fucked in the ass. Start jerking off. Imagine the younger hot mom letting me titty-fuck her. Just as I'm about to blow a load, hear Alyna knock on the door and ask if I'm "okay in there." Get nervous that I've been in the bathroom for too long and lose my hard-on. Turn off my phone. Assure her that I'm fine. Wash my hands and leave the bathroom.

2:46 P.M. Watch the five-year-old birthday boy unwrap a Wii console and complain that it's not an Xbox. Agree with the birthday boy.

2:52 P.M. Look at a giant framed picture of the birthday boy and his family hanging in the kitchen. Wonder how in the fuck Alyna knows this kid's mom. Wonder why in the fuck we had to come to this party. Wonder if this kid's mom takes it in the ass.

3:02 P.M. Get caught in a conversation with some kid's dad about the kind of pool he's having dug in his backyard. Wish I was dead.

3:03 P.M. Refill my Winnie the Pooh cup with chardonnay.

3:05 P.M. Almost knee some dipshit little girl in the face as I take a step and she runs past me as fast as she can, eyes closed, screaming about some other dipshit little girl taking her bracelet. Hope Jane never goes through the dipshit-little-girl phase.

3:06 P.M. Assume she will.

3:31 P.M. Find Alyna in the backyard with some other moms and younger kids. Act like I give a fuck about what any of them are talking about. Ask Alyna when this thing is going to end. Get a shoulder shrug. Head back

inside to see if any of the guys at this train wreck have
turned on a football game.

3:32 P.M.   Realize my only viewing options are *Toy Story 3* or
Dora the Explorer. Wonder if I could attempt jerking
off again. Find out the bathroom is occupied. Wonder
if it's another dad whose wife doesn't fuck him anymore jerking off while thinking about the young hot
mom.

3:38 P.M.   Wander back out to the backyard. Find Andy playing with a little girl in the grass by a swing set. Wonder
when he'll bang a chick for the first time. Hope the
chick is hot. Hope it's in high school or, at the very
latest, his freshman year of college.

3:47 P.M.   See some kid standing in the corner of the backyard by
himself. Notice that faraway look in his eyes. Notice
him make tiny fists. Recognize the look and actions of
a kid shitting his pants. Experience relief that he's not
my kid.

3:48 P.M.   Watch that kid's mom go over to him, raise him up,
sniff his ass, and then nod back at her husband, who's
standing up near the house. Watch the husband take
a long swig from his Winnie the Pooh cup.

3:50 P.M.   Take in the decorations in the backyard. *Toy Story*
balloons, a *Toy Story*–themed bounce house, a *Toy
Story*–themed ball crawl, a life-size Buzz Lightyear
statue.

3:53 P.M.   Try to remember having a birthday party like this
when I was kid. Can't. Don't think this type of shit
existed when I was a kid. Remember having a birthday
party as a tiny kid where two friends showed up and
we ate a pizza and watched *Krull* on Betamax. That
was it.

3:57 P.M.   Think about how weird it is that my kids won't even know what Betamax is. Think about how weird it is that my daughter might not even know what a CD or a DVD is. Wish I was a kid again.

3:59 P.M. Realize the party is wrapping up. Respond to Alyna waving me over to say good-bye to the hosts. Say good-bye.

4:00 P.M. Round up Andy.

4:01 P.M. Strap the kids into the car. Assure Alyna that I'm not too drunk to drive. Drunk-drive home.

4:17 P.M. Unstrap the kids. Jane is asleep. Take her inside with me. Lay her on my chest, still asleep, and sit down in the recliner to watch football. Watch a few minutes before I pass out, too.

8:34 P.M. Wake up slightly hungover and soaking wet. Realize that Jane has pissed all over me while sleeping. Call Alyna in to help me. She laughs at me, then takes Jane to the bathroom. Toss my clothes in the washer and head to the bathroom for a shower. Start to jerk off in the shower. Lose boner when I hear Alyna come into the bathroom and ask me if I can take some things to the post office for her on my way to work the following morning.

9:06 P.M. Tuck the kids in with Alyna. Give Alyna a back rub on our bed in the hope that it'll get her in the mood to fuck or suck my dick. Recognize the sound of Alyna snoring and realize she's fallen asleep during the back rub. Pull the covers up over her and go into the living room.

10:01 P.M. Watch the news. Want to fuck the news bitch.

10:37 P.M. Put hand in pants and tug at my dick a little but am too tired to get a hard-on. Give up.

10:40 P.M. Think about going to the office to jerk off to Internet porn but I'm too tired to get out of the chair.

10:42 P.M. Think about going to the office to jerk off to Internet porn but I'm again unable to conjure the energy to get out of the chair.

11:30 P.M. Watch Leno/Letterman.

12:30 A.M. Fall asleep watching Fallon.

1:07 A.M. Wake up. Realize I should go to bed. Reason that, if I have to get out of the chair, I should go to the office and jerk off to Internet porn. Stand up. Head to the office.

1:16 A.M. Blow load into a paper towel that I brought from the kitchen specifically so there would be minimal cleanup while watching Little Lupe take a dick in the ass. Start playing *Zuma* on Facebook.

1:32 A.M. Accidentally wake Alyna up as I get into bed. Tell her I was watching TV when she asks what I was doing.

1:48 A.M. Hear "I love you," say "I love you."

1:52 A.M. Welcome dreamless sleep.

chapter five

The Intern

I've already interviewed two potential interns—both huge douchebags. They're arrogant frat guys I could easily see turning into someone like my boss, Lonnie, in ten years. They talk about how exciting the world of business is to them and how much they just want to get in the game so they can start learning what it's really like outside of an academic setting. I know every word out of their mouths is bullshit. They just need internship credit for school, and the company I work for happens to supply it. They don't give a shit about anything. Neither do I, really, but I hope I don't have to choose one of these fucks to be wandering around the office every day asking me if there's anything they can do to be more productive.

After the second dickhead leaves the conference room, I check my schedule and see that the next candidate is a girl: Holly McDonnel. I look at her résumé, already knowing it will be identical to that of every other college kid I'll meet with. I notice she's twenty-one and immediately think about fucking her in the conference room. Even though I have no idea what she actually looks like, I imagine she has a young, hard body, no wrinkles, wearing a skirt that almost reveals the bottom of her ass but not quite. I imagine her telling me that she'll suck my dick if I can get her the internship. I imagine me telling her that she'll have to suck my dick or fuck me in my office once a week to keep it. I imagine her agreeing to my terms.

I leave the conference room and head to the lobby, where the potential interns are all waiting. Two more frat douches and a girl. She's fucking hot. Not exactly what I imagined but hot nonetheless. I say, "Holly?"

She says, "Yes."

I reach out my hand. She stands up and shakes it. I say, "Nice to meet you. Come on back," and let her walk in front of me toward the conference room.

She's shorter than I would have thought, maybe five foot two, and even though her skirt isn't as revealing as I previously hoped for, I can tell her ass is a little bigger than I would have thought from looking at her upper body. It's not big in a bad way at all; it's big in exactly the right way—just slightly too full for the rest of her body, which is skinny and slight. This makes her ass look even better. But it's tight. It's not tight from working out or running; it's tight from being twenty-one. It's the kind of ass that makes you grit your teeth because you can't help thinking about biting it. It reminds me of a slightly better version of Alyna's ass back when Alyna's ass was all I used to think about, back when it was great. I wonder if I'll ever get to fuck a girl with an ass like that again.

Her hair is pulled back in a tight bun, which is hot but not what I expected. I assume she's trying to look the part. And she's wearing glasses. I find this hot in a nerdy, librarian kind of way. I imagine looking down at her while she's sucking my dick and her looking back up at me through those glasses. I assume she has no episiotomy scar and she smells fucking incredible. She smells like melons and cinnamon. She smells like Alyna used to. She smells like something I want to put in my mouth.

I didn't do this with any of the douchebags before her, but as she sits down I ask her if she wants a glass of water or anything. She says she's fine. I started the other two interviews by asking them why they wanted to intern at our company and followed that with a standard list of questions that resulted in answers I didn't give a fuck about. With Holly, I decide to throw that out the window.

I say, "So, you from Los Angeles?"

She says, "Well, Chatsworth."

Without even thinking it might be inappropriate, I puke out, "Oh . . . porn capital of the world."

I immediately hope her response will put me at ease enough to not worry that I'll be sued for sexual harassment. She says, "Yeah. My mom is actually in the business."

I can't help myself, "Really?"

"No. I'm just kidding." She laughs. Her laugh is hot.

"You had me there for a second."

"Sorry. I know that was probably inappropriate."

"Not at all."

"Okay. Good."

"So your résumé says you write for the school paper."

"Yeah. It's fun. I've been kind of toying with the idea of being a writer, a journalist I mean, but that seems incredibly hard to make a living at, so . . ."

"So you're taking a bunch of business classes and that's why you're here."

"In a nutshell. I hope that doesn't sound bad."

"Not at all."

"Okay. Good. Because I'd really like this internship. I have a friend who did his internship here a few semesters ago and said it was really a great experience."

"What was his name?"

"Stanley Jimson."

"I can't say I remember him, but we might have put him in a department that I don't deal with all that much or something."

"Probably."

We stare at each other for a few seconds. There's no way I'm giving the internship to anyone else. She must sense that it's strange I'm not asking her anything. She says, "So, should I, like, tell you why I'd like this internship or anything?"

I realize I probably should make this interview seem legitimate, so that it's not blatantly obvious that I just hired the hottest chick I could find. I say, "Absolutely."

She gives the same answer that the two douchebags gave to the same question. It's almost verbatim. She says, "Well, I really think I could learn a lot about the business world here and I'd love the opportunity to see how a company like this works from the inside. I'm a hard worker and I don't mind doing anything that you guys would need me to do. No matter how small or rudimentary a task might seem to you, I'd view it as a valuable learning experience."

She keeps talking about some other shit, but all I can do is watch her lips move. They're not plump, they're not what I would consider traditionally good dick-sucking lips, but I can't stop imagining them on my cock. I'm still staring at her lips when I notice they haven't really moved for a few seconds at least and then she says, "So . . . yeah, that's why I would really love to be an intern here." I wonder if she realized I wasn't listening to her at all. I don't care. I say, "That's great. Great answer."

We stare at each other for a few weird moments. I'm wondering if she likes to get fucked in the morning when she says, "So . . ."

Wanting to give the illusion of legitimacy in this interview process, and also knowing that I'll be able to let her sweat it out for a week and then have an excuse to call her, I say, "Well, thanks very much for your time. We still have some other candidates to interview, but you should be hearing back shortly."

She says, "Sounds good. Thank you so much for having me in and I hope to hear from you soon."

We stand up, shake hands, and I open the conference room door for her and show her back to the lobby. I watch her ass move under her skirt the whole time. I want to fuck her. She leaves and I go through the motions with the other douchebags who think they have a shot at the internship.

After lunch I go to the third-floor bathroom and jerk off, thinking about Holly's ass and lips while I watch some college-coed porn on my phone. I imagine blowing my load on her tits, which I assume are hard and perfectly shaped.

chapter six

My Gay Buddy

I don't eat lunch with my gay friend Carlos as often as I used to before I got married and had kids, but we still get together from time to time. He sent me a very demanding e-mail this morning that said I had no choice but to have lunch with him today. He apparently has big news.

I'm sitting outside the Cheesecake Factory in Woodland Hills. The place is always packed at lunch hour with other shitty people doing shitty jobs that no one gives a fuck about. I thought talking loudly into your cell phone to seem important ended in the nineties, but there's a bald guy with a giant gut talking as loudly as possible into his Bluetooth earpiece about buying and selling something. I almost don't believe it's real until Carlos walks up and actually says to the guy, "Hey, nobody gives a fuck about what you're buying and selling on your fake phone call."

The guy is surprised and embarrassed. He walks off without saying anything. Carlos gives me a hug and says, "Long time no see, pussylicker."

"Yeah. The wife-and-kids thing. You know how it is . . . Oh wait, no you don't, you're a gay man."

"Fuck you. Let's eat."

We sit down outside, which I hate but Carlos insists on, and get some bread and water. I say, "So what's the news?"

He says, "Tedward and I are getting fucking married. Can you believe that shit?"

I say, "Wow. No. Where?"

"Not in California, obviously."

"New York?"

"Uh . . . no. I'm not a faggot."

"Uh . . . yes you are."

"No I'm not. I'm gay. I'm not a fag. Every fag in this fucking country is getting married in New York now. It was a cliché before it was even legal. Tedward has an aunt in Boston who has this gorgeous house she's going to let us use. It's going to be insane. And you and your brood are invited."

"We'll be there. When is it?"

"Four months from now. I'll send you the date and everything, but about four months from now."

"Shit, that's quick."

"It seems like it, but Tedward and I have been together for like almost five years now. Can you believe that shit?"

"Yeah, I guess."

The waiter comes to the table to take our orders. We order, and when the waiter leaves Carlos says, "I would put my tongue up his ass so fucking hard I'd be French-kissing him."

I say, "You better do it while you're still officially single. In four months that shit is over."

He says, "No. See, despite all of my best efforts, you still really don't understand how I operate, do you?"

"What in the fuck are you talking about?"

"Do you think I'd get married if it meant I couldn't get fucked by other guys?"

"So you're going to cheat on Tedward?"

"No, you fucking idiot. We bring a third party in all the time. Shit, sometimes even a fourth. Marriage doesn't mean the end of your sex life . . . unless you're straight. Thank god I'm not."

"Jesus."

"I've told you about this."

"You told me you had a threesome with Tedward *once*. I thought that one time was it."

"I don't know why I have to keep breaking it down for you in terms you can understand, but I will. If Alyna told you that not only was she cool with you bringing different chicks home for the two of you to have threesomes with, but she actually wanted you to because she liked eating pussy as much as you do, don't you think you'd be doing that pretty much as often as you possibly could?"

"Yeah, I guess I would."

"No shit. Well, Tedward likes to fuck . . . a lot. And I like to get fucked . . . a lot. So we find guys who want to fuck and get fucked and we're both happy as fucking clams."

"Sounds like a good setup."

"It is. And then, if we want to follow in your footsteps and have a family and the whole nine yards, we just go on the Internet and get a cute little Chinese baby. Which we don't, by the way. Kids are fucking disgusting and they ruin your life. No offense."

"None taken."

"So, that's my big news. I'm a bride to be."

"Well, congrats and welcome to the ranks of the happily married."

"Happily? So you're getting laid more, then?"

"I guess I meant welcome to the ranks of the legally married."

"You can't keep jerking off in the office."

"Yes I can."

"You always make me glad I was born to suck dick."

"I do what I can."

"When's the last time you fucked?"

"On my birthday and it wasn't even that good."

"You guys should be in couples therapy."

"You always say that shit."

"Because it's fucking good advice, asshole. I know you ruined your life with kids and shit, but you need to be fucking."

"Thanks."

"Anytime. If you want, I can give you the number of a good couples therapist."

"I'll pass for now, thanks."

"Suit yourself."

We order our food and eat. The rest of the conversation is about nothing important. We talk about movies and TV shows. Carlos tells me one of his clients just booked some huge but top-secret movie, and he's hoping that this client, who he explains loves him more than her own mother, will come with him when he jumps ship to a bigger agency like CAA or WME so he doesn't have to endure the humiliation of being an agent at Paradigm anymore. I tell him about the intern I'm going to hire. He laughs and tells me I'm pathetic.

He picks up the check, which he loves to do because it gives him a chance to use his black AmEx. He pays the bill and writes his phone number on the check, along with the following sentence: "Call me if you want the best blowjob you've ever had in your fucking life."

Reverse Grip

It's Saturday. We're in Toys R Us buying a birthday present for some other kid's birthday we have to go to that afternoon, which means I'll also be buying a toy for Andy and one for Jane. Can't fucking leave Toys R Us without shit for somebody else's kid's birthday and shit for all of your own kids.

I'm manning the shopping cart while Alyna has the kids somewhere in the store. As I answer a few e-mails on my phone, I hit the Internet app, which opens up the last page I was looking at—a video of a chick sucking cock on her knees. Although opening the video was an accident, I realize that I probably have a few minutes to myself, and I remember that the chick in it is hot, so I decide to mute the video and watch the rest of it while I wait for my wife and kids.

This chick is petite with blond hair and she has a great ass. She's cute in a way that isn't slutty. She really could be the girl next door. She reminds me in some way of Alyna when she was younger. I make a mental note of her name for future use: Lexi Belle.

As parents and children wander around me in the middle of Toys

R Us, I watch Lexi Belle gag on some guy's cock to the point that her eyes start tearing up. She's slobbering all over his dick with that slobber that you only see in porn, when the guy is really ramming his cock deep into the back of a girl's throat. It's got a higher viscosity than normal saliva. It's more like phlegm than spit. I'm not a fan of this kind of shit, but I keep watching. What else am I going to do in Toys R Us?

The guy is about ready to blow his load, so he rips his dick out of Lexi's mouth, takes one hand and pulls her head back with it, then takes the other hand and uses it to aim his cock at her face and starts jerking off. This is all pretty normal. The thing that is strange to me is the grip he uses. It's reversed.

The only way I've ever jerked off in my life is with my thumb and index finger toward the head of my dick. This motherfucker has the thumb and index finger toward his balls. It's fucking bizarre. Even Lexi Belle, who is paid to react to everything this guy does like it's the hottest thing she's ever experienced even if he's ripping her asshole apart, making her cry from gagging on his cock or shitting on her face—even Lexi fucking Belle can't hide a brief hint of surprised, mocking confusion when she sees this dude jerk off backwards and blow three giant white ropes across her eyes.

That night, after Alyna goes to sleep without touching my dick, I sneak into my office, cue up some POV porn of some Latina chick getting fucked in the ass, and try to jerk off backwards. I try for five minutes before I give up, not even close to cumming, and revert to the style I'm used to. I blow my load in under a minute, then slip back into bed wondering what strange events must have transpired in that guy's life to force him into jerking off backwards.

chapter seven

Holly's First Day

When Holly shows up for her first morning at work, I assign her to my department and give her a desk far enough away from my office that it won't be blatantly obvious what's going on but close enough that I can still see her if I wheel my chair slightly to the left and keep my door open. I've been staring at her ass for half an hour, trying to figure out some excuse to get her into my office, when an e-mail from my boss, Lonnie, pops up in my inbox:

> Accounts Receivable just released all of the financial
> statement hard copies. Can you get the new intern to tackle
> filing them in the library.

I fucking hate how Lonnie never uses question marks. I fire off an e-mail to Jeff Johnson in Records telling him to have those hard copies delivered to my office, and then I walk out to where Holly is sitting. She's fucking around on Facebook on the office computer, not even on her phone or anything—no attempt to be sly about it.

And as I walk up behind her she doesn't even try to minimize the window or log out. She sees nothing wrong with it and apparently doesn't care at all if I read everything on her screen. I wonder if she's just an entitled individual who sees nothing wrong with checking her Facebook at work, or if it's her entire generation. I try to imagine any of the guys who interviewed for the internship doing the same thing. It's extremely easy to imagine. This country is beyond fucked.

I say, "Holly?"

She turns around in her chair and says, "Yeah?"

"I've got your first assignment."

"Cool."

"Come into my office and I'll lay it out for you."

"'Kay, one sec."

She spins back around in her chair and actually finishes the message she was typing out on Facebook. It's something about a party to some guy named Tim. If she were actually an employee, not an off-the-charts piece-of-ass intern, I'd fire her on the spot. Instead, I wait for her to send the message and then watch as she leaves her Facebook page open on the screen, stands ups, and walks toward my office. She doesn't give a fuck who knows she was on Facebook and she doesn't give a fuck who reads her Facebook page. I'm baffled by this for a few seconds before I catch a glimpse of her ass that effectively erases my ability to think about anything else beyond what my dick would look like in her asshole and what color that asshole might be.

Once we're in my office, I notice her smell. That same cinnamon-and-melon combo that I picked up in her interview. I think back to fucking girls who smelled that good when I was younger and not washing the sheets until the smell wore off. I can't remember the last time Alyna smelled like anything other than Desitin and baby shit.

I say, "So this is not very fun or anything, but we have a bunch of stuff that's going to need to be filed."

She says, "Cool."

"The files are on their way to my office now, and when they get here I'll explain how they get filed and everything. It's not that complicated once you learn our little system."

"Cool. So should I wait here in your office for the files to come or go back to my desk?"

I didn't really think this out very well before getting her into my office. I just wanted some excuse to interact with her. I have no idea how long it will be until the files are delivered to my office, but I shake off the mesmerizing effect of how hot she is for a few seconds to remind myself that I'm technically her boss. She is my subordinate. I say, "Stay here. I guess we're going to be working together for the next few months, so let's get to know each other a little." As soon as I say it I feel like there's no way she could have taken it as anything other than what it actually is: an attempt to make her more comfortable with me so that I might eventually be able to fuck her. I imagine some variation of that same line has been used on her a dozen times by every professor she has at CSUN.

She says, "Okay. What do you want to know?"

I say, "You're from Chatsworth, right?"

"Yeah."

I realize that is the end of the conversation. She's twenty-one fucking years old. What else can I possibly ask her? What kind of interest rate she got on her home loan? A few seconds pass of me nodding my head and I'm about to ask her something ridiculous like what she likes to do on the weekends or if she lives on campus or not when I'm saved by our mail guy wheeling in two carts full of files.

I say, "Oh, well, there are the files. Guess it didn't take as long as I thought."

She says, "Cool."

I take a cart and she takes a cart and she follows me to the elevators. We go down to the records room, which used to be managed by this creepy old bitch named Cathy Fenner. She got laid off last year and now the records room is left unguarded. No one ever comes down here. As soon as we get off the elevator I start conjuring fantasies of fucking Holly in every possible location in the records room. I'm specifically imagining fucking her in the ass against the copy machine when we get to the accounts section.

I say, "Okay, here we are," and show her the six rows of filing cabinets where we've kept the hard copies of these records since before I started working here. I explain the inefficient filing system we use and file the first few with her to make sure she gets the hang of it.

I say, "Okay, I'm gonna head back up. If you need any help or have any questions or anything, just use that phone over by the copier and dial my extension—448. Other than that, just let me know when you're done."

She says, "Cool."

I take one more deep whiff of her before I head back to the elevator, knowing I'll be jerking off to imagined scenarios involving my dick in Holly McDonnel's ass tonight after my wife doesn't fuck me.

I dick around in my office for the rest of the day, watching videos of Bill Hicks and Joe Rogan on YouTube. At five-thirty, I notice I still haven't heard from Holly. I look out at her desk and she's not there. My first two thoughts are that she's been dicking off on her phone all day in the records room or that some guy wandered down there and got so worked up that he raped her. I know the probability of that second event happening is close enough to zero that my first guess is probably accurate.

I know Lonnie left at four-thirty, so I decide to fuck off half an hour early to go downstairs and check on Holly. When I get down to the records room, I find that neither of my two previous predictions was accurate. Holly's sitting in the middle of the two file carts with a few cabinets open, holding several files in her hands and crying. She's not sobbing, just crying a little. I assume she's gotten some bad news—a dead grandparent or a pet. I say, "Hey, are you okay?"

She looks at me with these big cartoony eyes that make me want to fall asleep with her while we're watching a movie on my couch and says, "Uh, not really, I don't think."

I say, "Do you need to leave? If there's an emergency or something, you can always leave if you need to."

"No, everything's fine emergency-wise. I think I just really messed up these files."

I'm stunned. How she could have fucked up this basic task is beyond me. The filing system, although completely outdated and inefficient, is nothing more than an alphanumeric code that gets filed in order of letter followed by number. My four-year-old son could probably do it. Beyond that, if she'd taken every one of these files and tossed them in the trash, no one would have known. Every file we keep is backed up digitally in a database, which is what everyone in the company uses if they need to find something. The hard-copy records room is just some bygone piece of protocol that the company refuses to discontinue. I suppose she has no way of knowing that, though. And instead of telling her I say, "Don't cry. It's fine. I'll help you and we'll get this done."

She says, "Really?"

"Yeah. It's no big deal," I say. "This system can be kind of confusing," I lie.

"I know. Thank you so much."

I take out my phone and text Alyna that I have to work late. She texts back, "k can you get dinner yourself?" To which I reply, "Yes."

I take Alyna's idea and say, "We'll probably be here for a few hours. Do you want to order dinner?"

Holly says, "Can we?"

"Yeah, we're working past six, so we get dinner."

"What can we get?"

"Anything you want that delivers around here."

"Is it cool if we get Stonefire?"

I find something endearing in her enthusiasm for getting shitty pizza instead of something from a decent restaurant in Woodland Hills. I say, "Yeah. If that's what you want."

I order a pizza and some salads and we start filing. As we file, we talk about nothing important. She tells me that she doesn't really know what she wants to do after college. She just wants to graduate and then figure things out. It's been so long since I was in college, I have nothing relatable to add to the conversation. I just listen. Eventually we start covering things like favorite TV shows and movies, though, and I find things to talk about. It turns out we're both big fans of *Tim and Eric Awesome, Show Great Job!* She accidentally lets it slip that she and her friends get high and watch it. Before she can apologize or retract the admission I lie and say, "Me too," in an attempt to put her at ease but also to make myself seem younger, cooler, more like what I imagine guys her age are like, more like what I imagine guys she likes to fuck are like.

We take a break when the pizza comes, and when I go to meet the delivery guy at the front door of the office I notice it's dark outside. For a brief second I feel guilty about having the conversation and the interactions I've had with Holly. I know Alyna would hate it. I know that, and yet I'm still kind of excited to go back into the records room and share a shitty pizza with Holly.

We eat and file and keep talking about innocuous things. She never mentions a boyfriend and I never mention a wife and two kids. An hour or so after the pizza is gone, I'm taking three or four files at a time and just cramming them into the file cabinets wherever they'll fit, knowing no one will ever come down here to look through them. With my new technique, we finish the job in another thirty minutes or so and then head back up to my floor to get our stuff and head out.

I walk her to her car, using the excuse that it's dark, and she says, "Thanks for walking me to my car. That's really sweet. And, seriously, thanks for helping me tonight."

"Listen, it was no problem. First days on new jobs usually suck. Hopefully I made it suck a little less."

"You definitely did."

We stare at each other for a few seconds. It feels like that moment at the end of a first date when you have to gauge what the girl is thinking and either move in for the kiss or not, but I know that feeling is probably only on my end. Then she says, "Would it be weird or against some kind of work rule for me to give you a hug?"

I can feel my dick getting hard just thinking about her tight little fucking body pressing up against mine. I say, "I don't think so."

She moves over and hugs me. It isn't a loose, barely-touch-the-other-person, end-with-a-pat-on-the-back work hug. This fucking hug is a here's-what-my-tits-feel-like-against-your-chest,here's-what-my-tight-flat-twenty-one-year-old-stomach-feels-like-against-your-older-less-flat-gut, here's-what-my-perfect-little-cheek-feels-like-brushing-against-yours, and here's-what-it-would-smell-like-if-I-was-fucking-you hug. I have to conjure every ounce of self-control I have not to squeeze her ass, and not because I'm so worked up by feeling her against me or anything, but because that hug makes her feel so familiar to me that it seems almost natural to let one of my hands slide down and get a little squeeze, like she's my college girlfriend or something.

I keep my hands where they should be and give her waist a little squeeze that I hope reciprocates but doesn't overstep the level of contact she initiated. We separate and she says, "Thanks again. See you tomorrow," then gets in her Mini Cooper and drives off.

I get home at nine-thirty or so. The kids are both in bed and Alyna is asleep on the couch. I can still smell Holly on me. I get in the shower and jerk off standing out of the stream of water so I can still smell her. After I blow my load I scrub down so that Alyna won't pick up any strange perfume, even though she'll probably be suspicious of me taking a shower, and I go back out in the living room. I wake her up by rubbing her feet. She says, "Oh, you're home. What'd you have to do that kept you so late?"

I say, "The new intern couldn't figure out our filing system so I stuck around to help."

She says, "Oh, that was nice. Did he finally get it?"

"Yeah."

chapter eight

Scheduling Castration

Alyna has been up my ass much more aggressively than usual lately
about getting a vasectomy. We both agree that two kids is the limit,
and she keeps claiming that she hates using condoms. I don't understand how she can even develop a hatred for something we only use
two or three times a month.

I'm sitting in my doctor's office on my lunch break. He's giving
me the phone number of a urologist friend of his who he claims is
the best at clipping guys' balls. I'm sure my doctor just gets a kickback
for every sucker he refers to this guy, but whatever. It seems like
a pretty simple procedure. I've heard of only a few mishaps where
vasectomies are concerned. My irrational fears of losing my dick or
testicles during the procedure give way to an even more irrational
thought: I find myself actually hoping that getting a vasectomy will
increase the number of times Alyna and I fuck per month. Then the
far more rational part of me chimes in and I realize I'm doing this to
placate her so she'll get off my back about it. And even if we still only
fuck a few times a month, at least I'll get to feel what it's like to have

my bare dick in a pussy again. That would excite me more if it wasn't Alyna's pussy.

Before I leave my doctor's office, I ask him if he's had a vasectomy. He's a little older than me and is married with kids. It makes sense to me that he might have. He laughs and says, "My wife's on the pill, thank god," without even realizing that this doesn't make me feel any better about the decision.

Once I'm back at work, I make a point of walking past Holly's desk a little closer than I should so I can smell her. She smells so good. I wonder if her pussy smells like that, if her asshole smells like that. I wonder what her mouth tastes like and assume it's probably like some kind of candy. I wonder what she looks like after she gets fucked hard. I wonder if she likes to cuddle after sex and what that might feel like if she does. I wonder when my daughter will start eliciting thoughts like these in men, and I wonder who the first man will be to have them about her. I hope that man is not like me but know that he most likely will be.

When I walk by Holly's desk she's on her Facebook page posting the lyrics to a song I've never heard as her status update. I don't recognize the lyrics or the band, which is called Rumspringa. I wonder if I'm too old to know the band or if they're actually just a bunch of guys she knows from college, all of whom I imagine are immense douchebags and at least one of whom I imagine to have fucked her because he's in the band and she is young and naive.

When I get back to my desk, I Google the band and find out that my first inclination was the right one, which surprises me. I listen to some of their music and find that I enjoy it. I try to remember the last time I heard a new band and can't. I wonder how that happened—how I became a guy who doesn't really care about music anymore, not even enough to attempt to hear new music.

I call the urologist my doctor recommended, assuming I'll be setting up a time to meet and talk with him about setting up a time to get a vasectomy. Instead his office tells me I can just set up a time to get the actual vasectomy. No discussion with the doctor is necessary for what they call "such a minor procedure." Despite the fact that I know there will be laser beams and possibly knives in my ball bag, this puts me at ease a little. I schedule it for the following month, allowing ample time to talk myself out of it should I need to.

After I hang up, I find some Rumspringa on the Internet and play it loud enough for Holly to hear. With luck, this will come across as a natural and coincidental display of similar interest, not as a transparent attempt to attract her attention.

I roll my chair out from behind my desk and to the left and peer through my open doorway to see if she notices. As I watch, she actually cocks her head up and back like a deer in the forest who's detected some faint but familiar noise. She scoots her chair a little closer to my office. I slide mine back to my desk before she can turn and look for the source of the music. I pretend to be working on something just in case my bait actually lures her into my office. It does.

She knocks on my door frame. I look up from my fake work—tracing over the logo on a piece of letterhead. She says, "Hey."

"Hey. What's up? More filing troubles?"

She laughs. She's hot. She says, "No. I think I got that down now, thanks to you."

"Glad to be of service." I want to be of several other kinds of service to her.

She says, "Are you listening to Rumspringa?"

"Yeah. Why?"

"They're like one of my favorite bands right now."

"Yeah, they're good."

"What's your favorite song?"

I glance quickly at the screen to see that a song called "Shake 'em Loose" is playing. I say, " 'Shake 'em Loose.' "

She says, " 'Shake 'em Loose Tonight'?"

I glance back at the screen and realize that the last word in the song title was cut off in the window where I had the song playing. I say, "Yeah."

She says, "I love that one. I really like 'Queer Eyed Boy,' too, though."

"That's a great one."

"Yeah. How'd you hear about them? They're not that big yet."

"Uh . . . you know. I'm into music. Always trying to find new bands and stuff."

"That's so cool. Have you seen them?"

"Live?"

"Yeah."

"No. I want to, but I never hear about their shows in time."

"Oh, I could totally let you know next time they're playing. They're local. Well, LA local."

"Yeah, that would be awesome."

She smiles. I can't tell if she's flirting with me or if she's had a sudden and unexpected realization that she's attracted to me or if she thinks it's funny that she has anything in common with a guy my age or if she's just young and hot and I'm reading far more into it than I should. Whatever the actuality is, she smiles and says, "Cool. I will." Then she turns around and goes back to her desk.

A few minutes later I get a Facebook friend request from her.

Facebook Stalking

I'm in my office at home. I log onto Facebook. I have forty-six friends. They are all actually my friends or at least people I know. Holly has 739 friends. I can't imagine they are all actually her friends or at least people she knows.

I have four profile photos: one of myself in a suit that was taken at work for my employee file, one of myself and my wife that was taken at the company holiday party last year, one of myself and my two kids that was taken by my wife in our backyard, and one of our entire family that Alyna hired a photographer to take about a year ago to be sent out as our family Christmas card. Beyond this I have a handful of other photos that I posted to my wall at various times for various meaningless reasons.

Holly has 324 profile photos and 2,543 other photos. I sift through the first twenty or thirty until I realize they're all essentially of three varieties: Holly taking a picture of herself from a high angle, Holly taking a picture of herself in a mirror, or Holly taking a picture of herself with a female friend in the picture.

My relationship status is "married." Holly's is "married" also. I click on her spouse and find it's another twenty-one-year-old girl, Megan Larrion. Holly is not actually married.

I scroll through the last twenty or so status updates she's posted. They're all from the last four hours. They range from "<3 New Girl <3 Zooey" to "Can someone please teach me to fly a plane?" They all have no less than fifty likes and no less than twenty-five to thirty comments, mostly from guys her age who don't even try to hide the fact that they want to fuck her, if they haven't already.

The post that really drives the nail in the coffin of my realization that I have nothing in common with anyone from this generation reads, "Can't find my socks!!!" The post has seventy-eight likes and fifty-four comments. Many of the comments are jokes—things like "Try looking on your feet. LOL!!!" or pieces of advice like "Just don't wear any!!!" But one comment by a guy with gouged ears and a lip ring named Tanner Dempsey, which reads "Holy crap! I lost my socks too!!!" actually gets Holly to respond.

Her response reads, "Oh noes! Where did you find them?"

Tanner's reply reads, "I just bought some new ones."

Holly's reply reads, "I don't have time to go buy new ones. Where should I look?"

Tanner's reply reads, "I guess in the dryer or something."

Holly's reply reads, "I did. There not there."

Tanner's reply reads, "You want to borrow a pair?"

Holly's reply reads, "They won't fit. LOL!!!"

Finally a guy named Tom Brown adds a comment that reads, "How can you only have one pair of fucking socks? LOL."

And that's the end of the thread. The degree of meaningless stupidity in all of her posts is beyond astonishing to me. I realize these are the things she's doing at work when she's on Facebook. I had imagined that she was sending out invitations to parties or posting links to articles about contemporary politics or world events.

The degree of physical attraction I have to her, and the fantasy relationship I've built with her over the few moments we've shared at work, make it far easier than I would have thought to dismiss all of this, to maintain my mental image of her as a smart and mature-for-her-age young college girl. I reason that I just must be out of the loop when it comes to kids her age and how they interact with one another. By placing too much importance on the hug we shared in the parking lot, I'm able to ignore the obvious fact that she's very probably the vapid type of young girl who needs attention from men so desperately that she's willing to spend hours on end fishing for men to give her that attention by constantly communicating her every thought and action on Facebook, including her missing socks. Just as I'm deciding that all of this is cute and innocent after all, my wife walks into our home office with her iPad in one hand and Jane in her other arm and says, "Who is Holly McDonnel?"

I log out of Facebook and say, "The new intern at work, why?"

"Why'd you friend her?"

"She sent me a request."

"Uh-huh. Is this the intern you told me was a guy?"

"I never said she was a guy."

"Yeah, I was under the impression the new intern was a guy, so you must have."

"What, are you pissed or something?"

"No. Not pissed."

I stand up and take Jane from her, in what I hope is a display of my loyalty to our family, even though I would love nothing more than to fuck the girl of whom my wife is now justifiably jealous. As Alyna walks away back into the living room she says, "She doesn't seem like the smartest tool in the shed."

I nod my head in agreement, then sit back down at the computer with Jane in my lap and log back on to Facebook. I look at Alyna's profile. She posts maybe one status update every three or four days, the last of which reads, "Watching some Yo Gabba Gabba with the kids." It has no comments and no likes.

chapter nine

Maria Reynaldi

Todd has a monthly poker game at his place in Hollywood. Alyna lets me go every four to six months. I never win money at these games, but I do take the opportunity to get drunk and complain about work and wives and kids with all of the other guys, who mainly complain about the same shit. Todd is the only guy at the game who isn't married with kids.

Todd says, "Done-zo. I'm a free motherfucking man, gentlemen. Kind of sucks, but also kind of feels fucking great. So, all of you married losers, let it be known that you're all on permanent wingman rotation."

A guy named Reggie Manning, who used to work with Todd, says, "You wouldn't want me as a wingman. I've been stomped in the cock so many times by my wife I don't think I'd even be able to talk to a chick."

Todd says, "Reggie, you should take notes from my man over here," and nods in my direction. He says, "This fucker's been married for what?"

I say, "Five years."

Todd says, "Five fucking years and the other night he was like a fish to water with these two sluts at Firefly. You should have seen it. Thing of fucking beauty."

I say, "It wasn't as crazy as he's making it out to be. We just had a few beers with these chicks. That was it."

A guy named Carl Cryzenski, who used to play in another weekly poker game with Todd, says, "Fuck, what I wouldn't give to have a few beers with some random skanks in a bar again. How often does your wife let you fuck her?"

I say, "Who, me?"

He says, "Yeah."

I say, "Probably two or three times a month."

He says, "I'm about the same. The shitty part is, though, she doesn't even want to. It's like she's obligated or something. I'd almost rather jerk off."

I realize that everyone sitting at this table is involved in a similar scenario except Todd. I wonder if the trade-off of having a family, having a woman and children you know will be there at your deathbed, is worth the price of sexual retirement in your mid-thirties.

Todd says, "You guys are a pack of fucking fags."

A guy named Lewis Carver, who I think is a friend of Carl's, says, "We're not fags for having families, dude."

Todd says, "Well, you talk like a pack of fags."

Todd laughs at this and tries to get the hand back on track by forcing Lewis, whom the action has been on for the length of this conversation, to bet or fold. He folds. Todd says, "You know what we should do instead of this? Seventh Veil."

Reggie says, "What's Seventh Veil?"

Todd says, "How long have you lived in LA?"

Reggie says, "I live in Toluca Lake."

Todd says, "It's the filthiest strip club of all time. Fully nude, so no booze. Or I think they serve beer or some shit now. But we should still get hammered here and then head over."

Carl says, "I told my wife I'd be sleeping on your couch anyway. I'm in."

I say, "Sure."

Lewis says, "It's only ten. I can't go home yet."

Todd says, "Ooh, the fags are growing some balls."

Lewis says, "Fags have balls, you retard. They fucking lick each others' balls and jizz all over each others' faces with the cum in those balls."

Todd says, "You know what I'm saying, douche."

Reggie displays visible signs of an impending anxiety attack as he makes his decision.

Todd says, "Reggie, what kind of tits does your wife have?"

Reggie says, "Pretty big. Why?"

Todd says, "Because the Veil will have a skank who has small tits."

Reggie almost gets a far-off look in his eye, like he's really thinking about some imaginary girl with small tits. He says, "I could be into seeing something like that."

Todd says, "Fuck seeing it. Twenty bucks will get it right in your face."

We all pound some shots of whatever shitty tequila Todd has at his place, and half an hour later we're drunk, paying our cover at the Seventh Veil. Once we're inside we all get seats next to each other around one of the stages, where a stripper who's easily forty-five bounces her ass up and down unenthusiastically as she watches the front door. Her tits are fake and enormous. This goes on for the length of Drake and Lil Wayne's "I'm on One," during which all the other guys get picked off by trolling strippers and make their way to the back room for private dances.

Then it's just Todd and me sitting out at the stage holding out dollar bills for the next stripper, who comes out and wipes down the pole with a rag. I notice that she's definitely too fat to be a stripper when I see her taking bills from customers by snapping them against the fat rolls on her hips with her G-string. As she snags one of my dollars in this manner, Todd says, "So, you miss this shit or what?"

I get another dollar out. "Not really, man. This is actually kind of shitty."

Todd points directly to the fat stripper's cunt, which she is exposing and spreading an inch from Todd's index finger, and says, "No, man. How is this shitty?"

I say, "I don't know. You know what I'm thinking about right now?"

Todd looks to the fat stripper, gives her a ten-dollar bill, and says, "Can you shut him up with your tits, please?"

I manage to get out the following as she smothers my face in her tits: "I'm thinking about my fucking kids."

She goes back to the stage and gets on her pole. Todd says, "But you're not thinking about your wife. Kids are something I'll never get, so I'll grant you that, but you wouldn't be in here right now if you were getting the right pussy from wifey."

I say, "Don't get me wrong, I'd love to fuck more, but we have kids. Fucking isn't what it's about anymore for us." Even as I say it, it sounds stupid. It sounds like something a guy like me is supposed to say to a guy like Todd at our age. I want to laugh at it, but instead I can feel something hot twisting and burning in the pit of my stomach. For a fleeting moment I think back to a time when I was with Casey, my girlfriend before Alyna. I remember one night after we got back from some art thing she wanted to go to at LACMA—some Gustav Klimt exhibit, I think. We hadn't fucked in a few days and I tried to initiate something by grabbing her tit and kissing her when we walked through her front door. She turned to me and said something about how our relationship didn't always have to be about sex. I remember how much I wanted to smash something when she said that, how much I wanted to scream in her face that our relationship was only about sex, that I would have no reason to ever hang out with her if she didn't fuck me. Relationships between men and women are *only* about sex. The rest of the shit is incidental.

Todd says, "Fucking is always what it's about, man. I saw you the other night. As much as you didn't want to fucking admit it, you were into those chicks flirting with us. I know you, man. Maybe you have some kids now, but there's the heart of a hunter in there, mother-fucker," he says, hitting my chest with the flat of his hand.

I say, "Those chicks wouldn't have fucked me."

Todd says, "Yeah, that one would have. Fuck her, though. You got any skanks at work or anything who are game? I know there's got to be some hot piece of ass running around that place who you just want to fucking gut like a fish."

I say, "There's a new intern."

Todd laughs and says, "There's that fucking hunter, strapping on his bow and arrow."

I say, "It's stupid. I'm sure she's not interested. And even if she was, I can't fucking cheat on my wife."

He says, "Why not? Who gives a fuck? Dude, listen up. My fucking dad told me this." I look at him quizzically. "You remember a few years back when he was really sick and shit and I had to go back home and take care of him and do the funeral and all that shit?"

I say, "Yeah," as the fat stripper rakes up her bills like leaves and a new stripper named Raven takes the stage. Raven is actually hot. Petite, pale, blue eyes, black hair. She has a tattoo on her ribcage in Latin: AUDACES FORTUNA IUVAT. She comes over to Todd and me at once. I assume it's because she saw us handing out bills to her fat friend. She spreads her legs to reveal a perfect pussy and asshole. I say to Todd, "Yeah, I remember."

Raven leans toward me and grazes my face with her perfect, hard, early-twenties tits. She smells like candy. Todd says, "Well, there were a few minutes on his last day when it was just me and him in his hospital room."

Raven whispers in my ear, "Hey, cutie." I can feel a hard-on starting.

Todd says, "My mom was out getting food or some shit and my sister was shitting or some shit. My dad fucking told me some shit."

Raven turns around and spreads her perfect ass. Todd says, "He started his little speech off by saying some bitch's name. He was like, 'Maria Reynaldi.' And I was like, 'Who in the hell is that, Dad?' I thought he was having dementia or something, right?"

Raven licks her own left nipple, looks at me, then smiles.

Todd says, "So he told me Maria Reynaldi was some bitch he had the chance to bang at some company Christmas party or some shit, but it would have meant cheating on my mom so he didn't fucking do it. He said that when you're on your fucking deathbed, like he actually fucking was—I mean, he literally died like less than a day after telling me this—he said, you don't give a fuck that your family is there. They don't stop the fact that you're dying. And he also said that the only thing you think about is fucking one last time, which you know you can't do. So you start thinking back over your life in terms of fucking—not about seeing your kid win some good-attendance award, not about the shit you did in your career, not even about shit like your wedding day or the day your kids were born, just about the fucking you did. And he said, you don't look back happily at the chicks you actually did fuck. He said, you're tormented by the ones you know you could have fucked but didn't because you were married or you didn't have the balls or whatever the reason might have been. He told me to fuck as many chicks as I could before I died no matter what. Even if I was married, had a girlfriend, or whatever, he made it real fucking clear that I should take every opportunity I could to fuck, so that the last thing that flashes through my brain before I die won't be some skank who got away like Maria fucking Reynaldi."

Raven's song ends. She leans over the stage railing and whispers in my ear, "You want a private dance?"

I say, "I'd like to, but I have to get back home to my wife and kids."

Todd says, "I don't have a wife and kids. I'll take a private dance."

I say, "Tell the guys I went home."

Todd says, "Pussy," as he and Raven head to the back room.

When I get home, everyone is asleep. I take a shower and get into bed. Alyna wakes up for a few seconds and says, "How'd poker go? You win any money?"

I say, "No. I lost forty bucks."

She says, "Sorry, honey," then goes back to sleep. I get out my phone and Google Raven's tattoo. AUDACES FORTUNA IUVAT. "Fortune favors the bold."

chapter ten

Maturity

I've been working on a proposal for exactly twenty-seven minutes and I'm ready to jump out my fucking window I'm so bored. I check my e-mail three times and then decide I need a real break. I get up and head to the kitchen, where I plan to spend at least ten minutes stirring two packets of Splenda into a cup of green tea while I think about fucking Holly. When I get to the kitchen, I find Holly there, talking to some kid we just hired in the mail room. He can't be older than twenty-three.

As I pass Holly, I say, "Hey."

She says, "Hey," back to me and then continues her conversation with this douchebag while I make my tea.

The douchebag says, "No, this place is seriously chill. You'll love it here."

Holly says, "How long have you worked here?"

The douchebag says, "I'm in my third month. Just doing that mail-room thing until I get promoted, which is probably going to be any day."

I want to kick this little fucker in his balls so hard he dies. Instead

I say nothing and take my hot water out of the microwave and drop a teabag in it. As I let it steep, I continue listening.

Holly says, "That's cool."

The douchebag says, "Yeah, I know. I figure I'll work here for a few years, work my way up that old chain, then bounce to a new place, get that salary bump and shit."

Holly says, "That's a good plan."

The douchebag says, "Yeah."

It's only at that point that I realize that neither of them is actually doing anything in the kitchen. They're not getting drinks. They're not making food. I can only guess this little shit saw her go into the kitchen for something and followed her in. Even though she's dicking off just as much as he is, I rationalize that she's only an intern, and immediately place the blame for their slacking on him. Nonetheless, I say nothing as I pour two packets of Splenda into my tea and start stirring as I listen to their conversation.

The douchebag says, "You should hang some time. Me and like four of my boys are renting this sick pad in the hills. We party up there constantly."

Holly says, "Five of you? How many bedrooms?"

The douchebag says, "Three. It's chill, though. Big bedrooms, and we have a sweet couch to crash on if one dude wants the room to himself for . . . you know, like if we have a chick over or something."

Holly says, "Cool."

The douchebag says, "Yeah, it's fly. So hook me up with your number and I'll text you when we have our next party."

Holly says, "You know what, I just switched phone numbers and I can't even remember what my new one is."

The douchebag says, "What's your e-mail then?"

I can't tell if he can't take a hint or if he's just a ballsy little fuck who won't take no for an answer. Either way, she caves and gives him her e-mail. He says, "Sweet, I'll hit you up," then leaves.

Holly turns to me and says, "I thought that guy would never leave."

I say, "Why'd you give him your e-mail then?"

She says, "To get rid of him."

I say, "He was kind of a douche, wasn't he?"

She says, "All guys my age are. They're just stupid little boys."

An irrational wave of images of Holly and me dating floods my head. I conjure scenarios in which she agrees to be my secret mistress. I imagine Alyna and my kids dying in a car crash and Holly being there to console me and eventually becoming my much younger wife. I feel immediately guilty about actually imagining my children dying.

I say, "You don't date guys your own age?"

She says, "I have, but I think I'm ready for a guy who's like a little older, you know? Like mature and everything."

I can't help myself. I say, "How much older are you talking about?"

She smiles and says, "I don't know, maybe like around however old you are."

I wonder if she can possibly imagine how hard I'm fucking her in the fantasy I've conjured of me ripping her skirt off and bending her over the table in the kitchen. I wonder if she knows that me thinking about her ass and pussy and tits is what has rendered me incapable of speech. I wonder if she knows exactly how to play me and that's what she gets off on. I wonder if she has no intention of dating a guy my age, of dating me. I wonder if the thought of us fucking repulses her. I don't care. It doesn't repulse me.

She says, "Well, I should probably go file some things or something. I've been in here a while."

I say, "Yeah," and watch her perfect ass bounce out of the kitchen. I sip my tea and wish I was young but hope she wasn't just fucking with me, because I am not young. I am mature.

Caught with the Babysitter

Alyna and the kids are in the backyard. She has filled up the little plastic swimming pool and they're fucking around, splashing each other and screaming. The kids like to do this on the weekends and it gives me thirty minutes to an hour of time when I don't have to deal with them. On this particular day, I decide to use my weekly allotment of free time to sneak into the office and jerk off. I haven't been able to jerk off during the middle of the day in a while, which seems like a special treat to me, and I also know that tonight I'll have to rub Alyna's back until she goes to sleep, and I won't want to manifest the effort necessary for me to leave our bed and sneak into the office to jerk off. So this is likely the only time in the next twenty-four hours I'll have free to blow a load.

I go into the office and drop the blinds that look out into the backyard. I can still kind of hear Alyna and the kids, which makes it a little weird, but I have no choice. I block them out and log in to NudeVista. com. I'm not in the mood for anything in particular, so I just click on the first thumbnail that looks good. It looks like a couple seducing a babysitter. Ever since we've had children, babysitter porn has become far more appealing to me than it ever was before.

I press PLAY on the clip and scroll through until I get to a part in which the young babysitter is riding the guy's dick while the wife, who's the same age as the guy, alternately licks his balls and the baby-sitter's asshole. I unbutton my pants, pull my underwear down a little bit, and start jerking off in my office chair. It takes me about forty-five seconds to get close to blowing a load, and then I hear from a few feet behind me, "What are you doing?"

A bunch of things happen at the same time that I have no control over. I just go into abort mode. I reflexively pull my underwear back over my dick, then close the window I had the porn playing in, then reset the browser history, then turn around to see Alyna with a dis-gusted look on her face and say, "Nothing, just some work stuff."

She says, "You were masturbating. I saw you."

I'm caught. There's nothing I can do. She's not being a good sport about this. I say, "Yeah. Sorry. I was horny."

She says, "Was that a guy and a babysitter or something?"

I say, "Yeah."

She says, "Are you into that?"

I say, "I don't know. It's porn."

As she stares at me like she walked in on me shitting into an ice cream cone and eating it, I try to imagine what it would be like if the roles were reversed. If I were to walk in on her fingering herself while she was watching porn, I'd go down on her instantaneously. I'd fuck the shit out of her until she came ten times. It would turn me on so much if I were to see her masturbating that I wouldn't be able to help myself. But Alyna is disgusted by it. She says, "Can you at least lock the door or something if you have to do that?"

If I have to do that. That phrase is all I can think about. She doesn't realize or care that I only "have to do that" because she has lost all interest in fucking me. But even if we *were* fucking, I'd still need to jerk off, because I'm a fucking man. I wonder if she wants to fuck other people or if she's lost interest in sex altogether. Somehow knowing that she just didn't want to fuck me specifically anymore would be easier to understand, but I don't think that's the case.

I say, "Why are you so pissed about this? We used to watch porn together when we first started going out. You used to have favorite actresses. You used to fucking bring porn home and suggest we do the shit the actors were doing."

She stands there not knowing how to react to this. The person I had to remind her she used to be is so far gone, she can't even conjure the memory.

She finally says, "Our kids are literally right outside the window," then walks out of the office and back into the backyard.

I sit there in my office chair, my hard-on softening, and look through the blinds. I see a woman who is disgusted by the sight of her husband experiencing sexual pleasure. I see my wife.

chapter eleven

A Ride Home

I'm closing down my computer at work and finishing a list of calls I need to make in the morning when Holly knocks on the door frame of my office.

I say, "Hey."

She says, "Hey."

"What's up?"

"Uh, I know this is probably like a serious hassle, and it's no big deal if you can't do it, but I kind of need a favor."

"Sure, what do you need?"

"I kind of need a ride home. My sister borrowed my car to go to Santa Barbara for some work thing this morning, and she was supposed to have it back by now but she got stuck up there, and all of my friends are doing stuff and can't pick me up and you're like the only person I really know here, so I thought I'd ask. And, seriously, it's no problem if you can't. I can just call my parents or something but I was trying to not have to deal with them."

I imagine her giving me a hand job while I drive. I imagine her sucking my dick while I drive. I imagine pulling over on the freeway and fucking her in the passenger's seat as cars speed by. I imagine smelling her pussy on my fingers the next day at work. I say, "No problem, just give me a few minutes."

She says, "Cool. Thank you so much," and then goes back out to her desk.

I sit back down at my desk and send Alyna a text telling her I'll be home a little late because my boss wants me to get some reports that don't actually exist ready for an early meeting tomorrow that will not actually take place. She texts back acknowledging my excuse and asking if she should leave dinner out or in the fridge. I respond by telling her to put it in the fridge and to kiss the kids goodnight for me if I don't make it back in time to tuck them in. I end by telling her that I love her, which is technically still true. She responds that she will kiss the kids goodnight for me and that she loves me, too. She ends her text by telling me not to wake her up when I get home because she is very tired and will definitely be asleep by ten.

The ride to CSUN is uneventful. There are no hand jobs. There are no blowjobs. There is no fucking. We talk about mundane things. She asks me about my family. I ask her about hers. There is no hint of the girl who openly flirted with me in the kitchen a few days before.

When we get to CSUN, she directs me to her dorm, which is slightly surprising to me. For some reason I thought she would have lived in an apartment. I pull up in front of her dorm and say, "Well, there you go. See you tomorrow."

I expect her to thank me and get out of my car. Instead she says, "Do you, you know, want to come in for a beer or something?"

My head floods with images of hand jobs, blowjobs, and fucking under the posters of Katy Perry and the vampires from *Twilight* that I'm sure must exist in her dorm room. I say, "Sure. I can stick around for a beer," then park my car.

She opens the door to her dorm room, and it's like walking into a solid wall of marijuana smoke. Her roommate is in the room, sitting on her bed and smoking pot from a bong shaped like a baseball bat. Holly says, "This is my roommate, Carly." Carly exhales a giant cloud of weed smoke and says, "Hey, dude." Carly is not initially attractive, but she is young, and although she is chubby I can tell it's a tight kind of chubby. She's plump, not fat. She's the kind of chubby that yields a fat ass that's extremely attractive in certain positions, I would assume.

Holly goes to a tiny fridge in the center of the room and pulls out two beers. She hands me one and then sits on her bed. The room is incredibly small. I haven't been in a dorm room since I was in college. I can either sit on the bed with Holly or sit at one of the two tiny desks at the foot of each of the beds. I say, "You mind if I sit on the bed with you?"

She laughs and says, "Uh, no . . . go ahead."

Carly says, "You guys want some?" and extends the bong toward us. Holly doesn't hesitate. She says, "Hells yeah," and takes a huge rip before extending the thing to me. I smoked pot a few times in college, but I haven't since, and even then I was kind of bad at it. Beyond that, I immediately fear Alyna smelling weed on me when I come home. Yet I reason that the damage is already done—I probably smell like a dispensary just from being in the room—and I don't want to seem like an uptight old guy to Holly, so I say, "Yeah."

I light it up and inhale a cloud of weed smoke that makes my mouth look like a window in a burning building when I cough it all back out. The girls laugh. My eyes are watering and my throat is burning. I take a quick swig of beer and start to feel high almost immediately. Holly pats my back and says, "You okay?"

I lean back on her bed and say, "Yeah. I think so. I will be." I laugh. This feels good. I look around her room. No posters of Katy Perry or *Twilight*. She has a poster of Christopher Hitchens with a halo above her bed and a poster of a band called Crystal Castles by her desk. The Hitchens poster surprises me and instantaneously buys back any of the vapid things she's said or posted on her Facebook page. There are a few scattered pictures of people I assume are her family. I hate Miller Lite, but the one I'm drinking tastes amazing.

She puts her hand on my chest and says, "Hey, really, thanks for the ride. My sister can be such a cunt sometimes." It feels good, in a way that's sexual and nonsexual at the same time. It makes me wish I'd had a pothead girlfriend in college, or at any time in my life really. Everything is so comfortable.

I say, "No problem. Thanks for . . . this."

She says, "For what?"

I say, "I don't know," and we laugh again.

Carly says, "So what do you do, dude? Are you like her boss or something?"

I say, "What do I do? What do I do?" I can tell I'm beyond high. The words make too much sense to me to make any sense at all. I say, "What do any of us do?"

Carly says, "What in the fuck are you talking about, dude?"

I say, "I'm not her boss, really. No one is. She's an intern. So I guess maybe, actually, everyone is her boss."

Carly says, "Dude, you're fucked up."

I say, "Yes, Carly, I am fucked up."

We spend the next hour or so talking about the universe and the possibility of alien life and parallel dimensions. When I ask about Crystal Castles, Holly plays some of their music and I find that I like it a lot. I don't think about Alyna or my kids at all as we leave their dorm room to go get frozen yogurt at a place on campus. I buy their frozen yogurt and we sit down to eat it. There are a few other kids in the place eating yogurt, too. I wonder if everyone in the place thinks I'm Holly's dad.

When we finish, I walk Holly and Carly back to their dorm room. Carly goes in by herself, leaving me and Holly outside. Holly says, "Thanks again. This was actually pretty fun."

I say, "Yeah it was. Thanks for the beer and the . . ."

"Weed?"

"Yeah."

She laughs. "Anytime."

We hug again. This time, even more than the last time in the parking lot, feels like the end of a date. We linger at the end of the hug, a little longer than the last time, looking at each other for a few seconds. She knows I have a wife and kids. I think she wants me to kiss her. I want to kiss her. I don't. I say, "Okay, see you tomorrow," and I give her one more quick little hug before I walk back to my car without turning around to look at her.

On the drive home, all I can think about is what she and Carly are talking about, if she's telling Carly how badly she wanted me to kiss her, or if they're laughing at me for being old and weird. I check Holly's Facebook page on my phone. She makes no mention of the night's events.

When I get home, Alyna's asleep. I put my clothes in a plastic trash bag, which I tie shut to conceal the smell of pot as best as I can. I check on the kids in their rooms, take a shower, and go to sleep wondering what in the fuck I'm doing.

The Romance Is Gone

I wake up. I get out of bed to take a piss, and when I get to the bathroom I look down and discover a giant log of shit nestled in a wad of brown-and-yellow-streaked toilet paper in our toilet. I know I didn't give birth to this fucking thing, and the kids never use this bathroom, nor could anything this size come out of one of their assholes. It had to be Alyna. She's still asleep.

I stare this thing down and it's peeking out of the water almost like it has a head, like it's staring back at me daring me to flush it, like it knows there's no way my toilet is strong enough to break it in half and suck it down, because it sure as fuck isn't going down in one piece. Something deep inside me doesn't want to flush it, anyway. Some greater sense of human justice keeps reminding me that it was Alyna, the same woman who bitched at me for jerking off, who brought this abomination into the world. This transgression cannot go without reprimand.

Before I issue a false accusation, I bend down and really look the thing over to make sure there's absolutely no way it could have been produced in one of my kids' colons, to make sure the blame for this inhumane act of disgusting bathroom etiquette could only lie with a fully grown adult human being. I know Jane can't even wipe her ass by herself, and Andy isn't great at it. There's no way the toilet paper that's with the turd would be that neatly wadded. It must be the work of an adult.

Is it possible that it was some other person? Is this evidence of a stranger in my bedroom? The cable man? Did Alyna fuck some other guy while I was at work, and did he fuck her so hard that he worked up a shit he chose to leave unflushed in my toilet to mark his territory? This seems pretty unlikely to me. I finally conclude that my initial instinct was correct. Alyna pushed out a burrito-size turd and just left it in the toilet without thinking about it, or perhaps left it there on purpose in some kind of passive-aggressive protest to something I've done. Either way, this must be addressed.

I wake her up. I say, "Alyna," and nudge her.

She wakes up and says, "What? Are the kids okay?"

"Yeah. Can you come look at something, though?"

"What?"

"Just come here."

"It's Saturday." She's clearly not happy about getting out of bed before she's ready to as I lead her into the bathroom and get her to stand directly in front of the toilet with the lid up.

She looks in the bowl and says, "So?"

I've worked this line up. I'm sure it'll get my point across. I say, "So . . . if you have to do that, can you at least flush?" putting as much effort as I can into mocking the tone she used with me when she caught me jerking off.

Either she doesn't remember saying the same thing to me, or she chooses to ignore my inflection. She flushes the toilet and says, "Sorry. Now can I get thirty more minutes of sleep, please," then walks back into the bedroom. I have to flush the toilet again to get the turd all the way down after she leaves, then I piss with the seat down and purposely splash some on the seat.

chapter twelve

Team Building

Lonnie walks into my office without knocking and says, "Gonna need you to knock out a little busywork."

I say, "Okay," assuming he wants me to reorganize some meaningless database that no one ever uses or something similar.

He says, "HR approved an interoffice team-building mixer this Friday. Applebee's. Need some flyers made up with Photoshop or something. Remember you being pretty good with those types of things."

I say, "Why wouldn't we just send out a company-wide e-mail?"

He says, "Nah. Flyer makes it seem more like a party, less like a work thing. Good to go?"

I say, "Yeah. Flyers. I'll take care of it."

Lonnie leaves and I look out my office doorway at Holly. I can tell she's on Facebook by how intently she's looking at her computer screen and how quickly she's typing.

It takes me about half an hour to make the flyer and to print out fifty copies, which I put up in various locations around the office. I make sure to save one to hand-deliver to Holly, who is indeed on Facebook when I walk up to her desk. She takes the flyer and says, "Ooh, Applebee's. Awesome." She's definitely being sarcastic.

I say, "I know. This company can be lame, but you get two free drinks."

She says, "Are you going?"

I say, "Are you?"

She smiles and says, "I might be persuaded into going if someone I know is going to be there."

"Well, then, I guess I'll have to go."

That night at dinner I tell Alyna that I have a mandatory team-building mixer for work on Friday night and I don't know how late it's going to go. She says, "They've been keeping you late more and more lately, and now they're making you do some seminar or whatever on a Friday night? You should ask for a raise or something."

I say, "It's not exactly a seminar, but yeah," just as Jane hits Andy in the head with a miniature carrot and laughs.

chapter thirteen

Professional Help

I'm sitting in my chair in the living room with Jane in my lap. We're watching an *Oddities* marathon. Alyna comes in with Andy, who's just had a bath, and initiates the following conversation in a whisper, which I can only assume has something to do with her not wanting the kids to hear even though they're in the room with us.

She whispers, "We need to talk about something."

I say in a normal volume, "Okay."

She keeps whispering. "I think," she says, taking a deep breath, "I think we should see a counselor," as she opens a bucket of Legos for Andy and dumps them on the ground.

I say, "What?"

Andy says, "I need wheels." She helps Andy sort through the mound of loose Legos for wheels and whispers, "I think we're having some issues right now. And I think a counselor might help."

I say, "Why are you whispering?"

She whispers, "Because the kids don't need to be involved in this."

Andy says, "Involved in what, Mommy?"

She says, "Nothing, baby. Here's your wheels," and hands him a few Lego wheels. Then she looks at me and whispers again, "So . . ."

I say, "So . . ."

She whispers, "Will you go?"

I say, "What issues are you talking about?"

She whispers, "You know."

I say, "No, I really don't."

She whispers, "Well, like me catching you doing you-know-what the other day."

I say, "I'm a guy. That's not an issue."

She whispers, "Yes it is. You shouldn't need to do that."

I feel like she's blaming me for jerking off even though she refuses to fuck me and I lose my shit. I say, "You're right. I have a wife. I shouldn't need to do that." This is the wrong thing to say.

She says, "Oh. So just because I'm your wife, I should be your personal sex slave?"

I say, "No, but maybe more than twice a month would be nice."

She says, "Well, it's hard with the kids. The whole world doesn't revolve around your crotch."

Andy says, "Mommy, do I have a crotch?"

Alyna says, "Not now, baby, play with your wheels." He does as instructed. I hope my son doesn't have to have a conversation like this one day with his wife in front of his kids—my grandkids.

I say, "Look, if you're not in the mood as often as I am, then you have to cut me some slack. I mean, it's my only fucking outlet."

She gasps in shock. She says, "Watch your mouth around them."

I say, "Sorry. But I didn't do anything wrong."

She says, "If you can't see anything wrong with what you did, then I'm scheduling an appointment for us to see someone soon."

I say, "Fine. Whatever."

She picks Andy up and takes him off to his room as he says,

"Wait, my Legos!" She comes back and scoops up the Legos into the bucket and takes it with them into his room, where they stay for the rest of the night. As Jane watches TV with me, I wonder what Holly is doing, and I wish I were back on her bed in her dorm room, high and happy.

chapter fourteen

First Taste

I'm sitting on a bar stool at the Applebee's in Woodland Hills, hoping Holly actually shows up to this shitty mixer. She wasn't at her desk when I left the office, so I didn't get a chance for any final confirmation. If she doesn't show, I'm going to pound my two free drinks and get the fuck out of here as soon as I can.

Most people blow these HR-sanctioned events off, but the usual crew that shows up to all of them is in attendance. Jim Treadwell from Accounting is sitting a few stools down from me. He's probably fifty, hates his wife, hates his kids, works late every night, drinks at Applebee's, Chili's, or Cheesecake Factory every night with anyone who'll join him. Stacey Primm from Legal is doing a shot and screaming, "Whooo!" like it's spring break and she's still in her twenties. She's probably forty, has one of those weird long asses, and just seems like she'd be terrible in the sack. I wonder if anyone at work has fucked her and would be willing to fill me in. Randy Burke, also from Legal, is trying his hardest to be funny by yelling, "Next round's on me, guys," and holding up a drink ticket. No one laughs. He got caught chatting with a cam girl in his office last year, but it was after hours, and it was on his iPad instead of company property so he just had to take sensitivity training. He didn't get fired, but everyone knows he was jerking off at work, which might be worse than getting fired. And Wendy Brills from HR walks up to me with her three chins and hands me my two drink tickets as she says, "Nice turnout. Thanks for making the flyers. I'd love to give you an extra drink ticket, but rules are rules."

I take my drink tickets and use them to order two double J&Bs on the rocks from a cute waitress. I imagine fucking her in some back room or office that must exist somewhere in the Applebee's. When she brings the drinks back, I pound the first one and plan on doing the same to the second when I feel a hand on my shoulder and hear Holly say, "Slow down, cowboy."

I leave the second drink on the bar and turn to look at her with a smile on my face, but she's not looking at me. She's looking down at her phone, texting or updating her Facebook status or something. My smile fades away during the ten awkward seconds it takes her to finish whatever she's doing on her phone. Finally she looks up and I put the smile back on. So does she. When she hugs me, when she presses those hard titties against my chest and rubs my lower back with more pressure than a casual work acquaintance should, I don't give a fuck about the ten seconds she ignored me. I say, "Hey. Glad you showed up."

She says, "I told you I was going to if you were going to."

"Yeah, I know. I just didn't see you before I left the office, so I didn't know."

"I'm a woman of my word."

"Fair enough."

"So how would I go about getting some of those drink tickets?"

Wendy is still a few feet away. I say, "Wendy, can Holly here get a few drink tickets?"

Wendy turns around and says, "Oh, sorry, we're only authorized to give tickets to full-time employees. Interns don't count."

Holly looks at me with an exaggerated pouty frown and sad eyes. I say, "Here," and slide her my other double J&B. She pounds it without batting an eye and says, "Okay, I'll get the next round if you get the one after."

"I'm game."

For the next three hours we talk about a lot of things, none of which is my wife and children. She never leaves my side to talk to anyone else, nor does she stop texting or checking her Facebook for more than a minute. Nonetheless, we drink, we order appetizers, we get to know each other. Even though I'm positive she must know I'm married, it feels like a date.

As the Applebee's staff initiates last call just before midnight, I look around and see that everyone from work has left, except for Jim Treadwell, who is polishing off what has to be his seventh or eighth screwdriver. Out of obligation I say, "Hey, man, you need a cab or a ride or something?" He looks at me and says, "Nah. My drive home is the last time I'll have alone," pounds his drink, unenthusiastically tosses a few bills on the counter without even waiting for his tab, and leaves. I can see myself becoming Jim Treadwell in fifteen or twenty years.

I say to Holly, "Last call. You want another one?"

She says, "No, I'm seriously hammered as it is. One more and I'll be puking."

"Do you need a cab or a ride or something?"

She looks up from her phone, smiles, and I think I detect some flirtation in the way she says, "Mmm, a ride home sounds like it could be fun." I pay our tab and we walk out into the parking lot. She doesn't seem that drunk to me until she stumbles and almost falls near my car. I put my arm out to help her get her balance. She laughs and says, "Almost ate shit. That would have been embarrassing."

I open the passenger's-side door for her and she gets in. As I walk around to the other side, all I can think about is what her ass must look like naked. I get in the car, start it, and reach for my seatbelt. Before I can click it into place, Holly says, "Hang on before you do that." Then she leans over and kisses me.

My brain is on fucking fire. Her lips are so wet and young and she tastes like fucking Life Savers and bubble gum and booze. It's a hundred times better than every time I've imagined it. Once I get past the initial lobotomy her kiss delivers to me I start remembering things. I have a wife. I have kids. That wife and those kids are at home, expecting me to be in that same home in the next thirty minutes to an hour. I pull back from her.

She says, "What's wrong?"

I say, "I don't think I can do this."

"Yeah, you can."

"Really, I don't think I can."

She takes my hand and slides it up her leg under her skirt, straight to her pussy. Her legs are smooth and tight and she's not wearing any underwear and her pussy is wet. She says, "See how wet you're making me? You can't just leave me like this."

The hard-on I get from this could dent a beer keg. She says, "So . . ." as she pushes my index finger into her pussy. It feels like a Chinese finger trap. Alyna is in my head telling me we need to go to therapy. My kids are in my head asking me why I came home so late. And ultimately Todd is in my head reminding me about Maria Reynaldi. I try to project myself into the future. If I don't fuck Holly, will she become my Maria Reynaldi? Will I become Jim Treadwell at the end of the bar, doing anything I can not to have to go back home to my shitty family? Does Jim Treadwell have a Maria Reynaldi? Is that why he's so fucking miserable?

Fuck it. I lean in and kiss her hard, pulling her mouth to mine. I rub her clit a little and whisper, "Is your roommate gone?"

She says, "Let's just fuck here."

I say, "In my car?"

"Yeah, let's steam up these windows."

It's a terrible idea. I haven't fucked in a car since college. I say, "Okay."

We climb into the back and lay the seats down as far as they'll go. It's cramped, but it doesn't matter. Without wasting any time, she unzips my pants and starts sucking my cock with an urgency that makes it seem like the world's going to end if she doesn't have my dick down her throat. She's not great at sucking cock, but she does it like a porno movie. She spits on it, strokes it, then crams it down the back of her throat until she gags and her eyes water. It could feel better, but the enthusiasm is hot as fuck to me. I grab her hair and pull it just a little as she sucks my dick. She says, "Yeah, fuck my mouth." I do.

After a few minutes, she comes up for air and says, "Fuck me." I realize I haven't even thought about rubbers. I know I don't have any but I don't care. I've already committed. If I have to fuck her without a rubber, I'll just pull out and hope she doesn't have herpes or AIDS.

She straddles me and hikes her skirt up a little, then reaches over to her purse and fishes around until she finds a rubber. This both relieves and alarms me. She's clearly a slut if she's carrying around rubbers in her purse just in case, but at least she's a safe slut. She unwraps the rubber and rolls it onto my dick, then she moves her hips around and slides my cock into herself. Even with the rubber, I can tell her pussy is the tightest one I've probably ever had my dick in. I immediately wonder if this could possibly be true. How could it be tighter than my high school girlfriend, who was a virgin? I reason that it's just in comparison to Alyna's pussy, which has had two kids stretch it out beyond repair.

I reach around and grab her perfect ass as she rides my dick. She pulls the front of her shirt down so one of her tits is exposed, then reaches around the back of my head and pulls my mouth onto her nipple. She moans when I start sucking on it.

We fuck like this for about five minutes before she says, "Give me your finger." I extend an index finger toward her. She takes my hand and sucks my finger, coating it in her saliva, then says, "I'm about to cum—stick it in my asshole."

I say, "My finger?"

She says, "Yes."

I slide my finger into her asshole. It makes her pussy even tighter. I think I can even feel my dick with my finger through her asshole. She says, "Yeah, that's it. Now fuck me hard."

I fuck her as hard as I can in the confines of my car. A minute later she moans louder than she has before and says, "I'm cumming. Oh god, I'm cumming." Her whole body starts shaking. The realization of what's happening starts sinking in. I have my finger in a twenty-one-year-old's perfect asshole, my dick in her perfect pussy, and she's cumming all over it. I blow my load instantaneously. We cum together.

She falls down on top of me, breathing heavy. She's sweaty. Her hair smells great. I kiss her on the neck. She's salty. I look at the ceiling of my car, and for a second I don't think about Alyna and my kids. For a second I'm just happy.

Holly sits up and gets off my cock. She says, "That was seriously hot."

"Yeah, it was."

"Wow. I thought you would probably be good at fucking. I was right."

"What made you think that?"

"The way you're always looking at me like you want to fuck me."

"You've noticed that?"

"Yeah, it's hot. So glad I was right about you being able to fuck."

"Well, you're not too bad yourself."

"Really? Did you like it?"

"Uh, yeah . . . were you not here?"

"Yeah, I obviously was, I just want to make sure you liked it."

"I did. A lot."

I look down at my shrinking dick in a rubber full of cum. I don't really know what to do with it, so I roll down my window and fling it out into the parking lot. I've seen dozens of used rubbers in parking lots, and I always wondered what kind of animal would just toss a used rubber on the ground, what kind of a scenario would warrant such an action. I now have my answer.

I wipe my dick off with a blanket I have in the backseat and then toss it under the driver's seat. We get out of my car, and Holly starts heading toward her car. I say, "Hey, don't you still need a ride?"

She says, "No, I'm fine. I'm not even drunk. I just wanted to fuck you."

My ego couldn't be any bigger. I say, "Oh, well, oh. Okay."

"So, I'll see you at work tomorrow?"

"Yeah."

She gets into her car and drives away. I sit in the parking lot of Applebee's for a few minutes, mentally preparing myself for dealing with Alyna. I reason that it's doubtful she'll suspect that this kind of thing could have happened, so she won't ask any direct questions. She'll probably be asleep, so I won't have to deal with her at all, which would be the best-case scenario. But if she is awake, I'll have to do some tap dancing to be able to get into the shower without suspicion. I contemplate calling Todd and asking him if I can shower at his place, but that would double my drive time back home. I decide to take my chances.

As I drive out of the parking lot, I think that, even if Alyna catches me, it was worth it, because I got to feel what it was like to be truly alive one more time.

When I get home, everyone's asleep. I put my clothes in the washer and start a load. I take a shower. I sniff my fingers one last time before washing off the smell of Holly's pussy and asshole. I crawl into bed next to Alyna without waking her up. I feel guilty, but the memory of Holly licking my finger before asking me to put it in her asshole makes me feel much better.

chapter fifteen

The Morning After

I'm not as anxious as I thought I'd be around Alyna and the kids. I certainly feel as guilty as I imagined I would, but I don't feel anxious. No part of me thinks Alyna will ever find out that less than ten hours ago I had my dick in my intern's pussy and my finger in her asshole literally right where our children are sitting as I strap them in for a trip to see *Brave*, which looks like an even bigger steaming pile of shit than most movies I'm forced to pay for and sit through at the behest of my children.

As I click Andy's seatbelt he reaches out and digs at something on the back of the driver's seat and says, "What's this, Daddy?" I turn around and see that he's trying to scrape off a spot of what can only be my dried semen from the night before. It must have been an errant drop that found its way out of the condom when I flung it out of the window. I can feel my intestines twisting into knots.

I say, "That's just some dirt or something, bud," as my mind frantically races through every possible fucking thing that could have been left in the car in the aftermath of a rushed fuck with a twenty-one-year-old the night before. I mean, if my fucking cum is on the back of the seat, Holly's dirty thong could be hanging off the rearview mirror. I do as thorough a scan of the backseat as I can without drawing too much attention from Alyna, who is sitting in the passenger's seat reading something on her phone. As I click Jane into her car seat, I look under the front seats for any errant hair clips, earrings, or other things I would never be able to explain away. I see nothing and hope I'm not missing anything.

I pop back up from the floorboards and see that Andy is really digging away at my dried cum. It's like he's one of the guys at the car wash detailing my car or something. I know that, at some point while I'm driving, he's going to scratch some off and put it in his mouth. That's what kids fucking do. I won't be able to stop it. It should seem far more disgusting than it does to me, but I chalk it up to the fact that my immediate concern over getting caught fucking another girl is far more pressing than worrying about the implications of my four-year-old son touching and possibly eating my dried semen.

For the entire drive to the theater I can hear and feel Andy scratching away like a little fucking gerbil. Luckily Alyna never really pays his little excavation much attention. I imagine her inspecting the spot close enough to smell it and identify it as semen. I concoct an elaborate excuse that involves me having to masturbate in the car because she got pissed the last time I did it in the house. I assume she'd buy the bullshit excuse after finding me jerking off to babysitter porn. It might result in me having to undergo voluntary sex-addict counseling or something, but that beats getting caught cheating.

When we get to the parking structure, I get Andy out first and look at the spot where my cum was. There's still a little white crusty spot, but it's about a fourth as big as it was when he started scratching at it, and he's biting his index fingernail. I am a terrible father.

Sexting

I'm sitting in my chair watching a recorded episode of *The Soup*. Alyna and the kids are asleep. It's 11:43 P.M. My phone buzzes and I see that I have a new text message. It's from Holly and it reads, "I can't stop thinking about last night. I love your cock."

Other than the immediate involuntary reaction of starting to get a hard-on, I have no idea what to do. I know sexting is the focus of a segment on local morning shows every other week, and plenty of people get caught sending pictures of their genitals to people they're fucking, but I've never experienced any of that, because I've been married for the entirety of the techno-sexual revolution.

My first instinct is to reply with a text that reads, "Thank you," but that can't be right. I think it's probably better to respond with something equally sexual, something that conveys my interest in fucking her as well. I type out, "Your pussy is incredible." It looks wrong. I read it out loud and it sounds even worse than it looks. I start to think I'm taking too much time to respond. I wonder if she's been fingering herself since she sent me the text or if she's just out with her twenty-year-old friends trying to get me to reply with something stupid so she can show them. I immediately discount the last thought and rationalize it away as false insecurity by reminding myself that she actually fucked me. Not only did she fuck me, she gagged on my cock and forced me to put my finger in her asshole. She's into this.

I think briefly about texting something like, "I really liked my finger in your asshole," but that sounds too nice, almost clinical. It's not dirty or visceral enough to carry the same level of sexual desire as her text. I wonder if I should play it cool and respond with a question like, "Yeah? What do you love about it?" I type it in and read it over. It doesn't sound as bad as the other shit, and it seems to put me in some position of power in the conversation, without having to use profanity or vulgarity, which seem awkward in a text message. I send it.

A few seconds later she replies. "It's big and hard and I love the way it feels in my wet little pussy. Does that turn you on?"

I have a hard-on before I finish reading the text. I contemplate replying by letting her know that, but instead opt for telling her, "Everything about you turns me on."

She replies with a text that reads, "Carly's at the library and I'm fingering my pussy right now on my bed and thinking about you fucking me from behind," which starts me imagining what her perfect little ass must look like doggy-style. I wonder if her asshole is the same color as her skin or if it's darker. Either way, I realize that I want to see it badly. Seeing it means I'm going to have to fuck her again. Fucking her again means I'm going to have to cheat on my wife again. I wonder if I can cheat on my wife again, and if I can, what that will mean. I know that if I do it again, I'll be able to do it several more times after that. I assume it will become a full-blown affair and I'll have to start leading a double life, which has to be a difficult thing to do.

I type, "Holly, we can't do this," then stare at the text, knowing that a little farther up the 405 in a dorm room at CSUN the hottest girl I've ever fucked in my life has her finger in her perfect little pussy and she's texting me—not some douchebag her own age—the dirtiest shit she can think of.

I erase it and type in, "Is that how you want me to fuck you next time?"

chapter sixteen

Open and Honest

Alyna and I pull up in front of a small house in Burbank. We've left the kids with her friend Isabelle. I say, "This guy doesn't operate out of an office?"

She says, "This is his office."

"This is a house."

"It's a home office."

We get out and walk up to the home office of a couples therapist for our first session. When we get to the porch, I reach up to ring the doorbell. Alyna grabs my hand and says, "Hey, what are you doing?"

"Ringing the bell."

She points to a sign hanging from the doorknob that reads, SESSION IN PROGRESS. PLEASE TAKE A SEAT UNTIL IT CONCLUDES AND RESPECT MY CLIENTS BY NOT RINGING THE DOORBELL OR KNOCKING. THANK YOU. ROLAND.

I notice two white plastic lawn chairs sitting on the porch, which I assume are meant for us. I can't help saying, "This guy seems real legit."

Alyna says, "He is. Rachel and Doug have been seeing him for a year now and they say he's really helped them."

"Couldn't have helped much if they're still seeing him after a year."

"Will you at least give this a chance? Please, for me, can you just not make jokes and treat this seriously?"

I look at Alyna and wonder if Holly will ever be married to a guy she forces into couples therapy. Even though I had my finger in her ass, somehow it seems likely to me. I say, "Calm down. Yes. I can take it seriously."

She says, "Thank you," and sits down in the lawn chair next to me.

After a few minutes of silence, the door opens and a couple comes out. The guy looks like someone just spent an hour kicking him in the ball bag, and the chick has a giant smile on her face. Eye contact with everyone on Roland's porch is unavoidable. We all nod to one another. The guy gives me a nod that silently says, "You have no idea what you're in for, you poor fucking bastard." The chick gives me a nod that silently says, "I know you're a fucking asshole or your wife wouldn't have had to bring you here." Alyna gets a nod from the chick that silently says, "You go, girl." And she gets a nod from the guy that silently says, "Fuck you, cunt." They leave and walk off toward their car as Roland says, "Alyna?"

She says, "Yes. Nice to meet you."

He says, "You, too. Thanks for being prompt."

She says, "Well, the babysitter gets paid by the hour," and they both laugh a forced laugh. All I can think is, this motherfucker gets paid by the hour, too, and I'm sure his rate is about ten times what I'm paying the fucking babysitter.

We walk inside Roland's house and he takes us to his second bedroom, which he's converted into an office for therapy. There are three chairs. Alyna and I take the two that are clearly for the couple seeking therapy, and Roland takes the one that faces us both. He takes out a little journal in a leather jacket and an overly fancy pen and says, "Okay, you guys, you obviously wouldn't be here if things were as good as they could be in your relationship. And that's how I want you to think of it, too. Too many couples think of couples therapy as something you do when there's a problem in the relationship, but that's not what this is about. This is about helping you guys get every-thing out of your relationship that you can, even when things are going fine. So I'll ask each of you, without wording it in a way that makes it sound like a problem, what is one way you'd like to see your relation-ship improve? Alyna, why don't you start?"

She says, "Okay. I'd like to catch my husband masturbating less frequently."

I say, "Jesus Christ. Does he have to know that?"

Roland says, "It's okay. I don't judge anything that's said in this room, and I need you both to be open and honest for this process to work. Okay?"

Alyna says, "Okay."

I say, "Fair enough. If we're putting it all out there, the reason I was jerking off—"

Alyna cuts me off. "Can you say *masturbating*, please?"

I say, "Fine. The reason I was masturbating is that my wife will only fuck me twice a month, if I'm lucky, and she doesn't even seem to be interested in those two times while they're happening."

Alyna stares at me with her mouth open. "Can you say *making love*, please?"

Roland leans back in his chair, puts his little journal down on the ground, and says, "Okay, guys. This is a very common issue in mar-riages, especially after kids are introduced. It's tough to maintain that same level of physical intimacy that you had in the beginning of the relationship when you have to worry about dirty diapers and trips to the pediatrician and rides to school. So what I'll ask both of you to do right now is be extremely honest with one another and promise each other, and me, that you won't react emotionally to anything that's said over the next hour but instead you'll hear everything and process it logically. Can you do that?"

I say, "Yeah."

Alyna says, "Of course."

Roland says, "Good. So, Alyna, you start again and tell your husband one thing that turns you on about him."

I can't fucking believe what I'm hearing. Roland is a fucking genius. With one sentence, it's like he's erased every complaint in Alyna's head. As I wait for her to say something, to say anything, I know the real answer is that *nothing* about me turns my wife on.

She says, "Well, you really are a good provider for us. For our family, I mean. You work hard." This is a total crock of shit. Alyna's just throwing out some generic compliment in an effort to completely avoid actually answering the question, actually addressing the matter at hand. I want Roland to nail her to the wall for it.

Roland says, "And this sexually arouses you?" Roland is my new best fucking friend. I love this guy.

She says, "Well, not sexually, but it's an attractive quality."

Roland says, "Well, can you think of something about your husband that *sexually* arouses you?"

She says, "This isn't a fair question. We have two kids. We've been married for five years. I mean, can he name something that sexually arouses him about me?"

Without hesitating for a single second I say, "Your ass, your tits, the sound you make when you cum, the way your neck smells, the way your mouth looks when you eat marshmallows, and the taste of your pussy," and I sit there staring at her, waiting for her to have anything to say in response to this. She just stares at me. She knows I'm being honest, and she knows she can't even come close to my answer.

Roland says, "Alyna, how does hearing that make you feel?"

Alyna says, "I feel a little embarrassed, actually."

Roland says, "Why?"

She says, "Because I just don't see myself like that anymore, I guess. I'm a mom now."

Roland says, "But before you were ever a mom, you were a woman your husband was very attracted to, and obviously still is."

Roland spends the rest of the hour giving us pointers on things we can do to increase the frequency with which we have sex. When we leave Roland's home office we walk past another couple sitting in the plastic lawn chairs. The guy looks like he'd rather be drinking from a fountain of liquid shit than sitting on that porch until he sees that I have a giant smile on my face and Alyna looks like someone spent the last hour kicking her in the cunt.

chapter seventeen

Nooner

Holly walks into my office at twelve-thirty on Monday and says, "What are you doing for lunch?" It's the first time I've seen her since fucking her in the backseat of my car on Friday, and it's the first time I've communicated with her in any form since she texted me the play-by-play of her fingering herself in her dorm room on Saturday night.

I say, "I have no plans. You want to grab something with me?"

Forty-five minutes later we're in her dorm room at CSUN and my dick is in her ass. She's riding me reverse-cowgirl-style and moaning as she says, "Don't cum in my ass. Save it."

I say, "For what?" as she answers my question by spinning around and sucking my dick until I fire a mess of cum all over her face and mouth. She giggles a little as I do, then she opens her mouth and shows me the cum on her tongue for a few seconds before she swallows it and says, "That was so fucking hot." She keeps sucking my dick until it goes completely limp and then crawls up next to me and puts her head in the crook of my arm.

I go over a mental checklist of the shit that just went down, making sure I'm remembering it accurately, making sure I won't forget a single detail later when I'm jerking off while Alyna sleeps.

When we got in my car forty minutes ago, I was expecting to go to Chili's or something. She said, "My roommate has class until two. You want to fuck me in the ass?" I drove to her dorm room doing eighty miles an hour. We walked in, she gagged on my dick for a minute, then forced it into her ass using only her own saliva as lube. Then she sucked my dick again until I blew a load immediately after it was in her own asshole.

Once I have it all straight in my head I say, "So . . . don't take this the wrong way, but where did you learn to do all of that?"

She says, "Do what?"

I say, "The stuff you do during sex?"

She says, "What do you mean? Do I do something weird or something?"

I say, "No, no, no. I don't mean it like that at all. I fucking love everything you do. You just . . . well, you have sex like it's a porn movie or something. Again, I love it. I'm not complaining, I'm just curious. That's all."

She says, "Is there some other way to have sex?" And it hits me: She's twenty-one. When she first got curious about sex in junior high, she didn't go to her mom or to *Cosmo*, she went to the fucking Internet. Everything she knows about sex came from watching porn because she grew up with instant access to it. It dawns on me: It's not just Holly. Every girl her age probably learned about sex by watching porn. And they probably all fuck like they're in a porn movie. I wonder if Holly actually enjoys getting fucked in the ass, or if she just thinks that's a normal part of sex because it's in virtually every porno movie she's ever seen.

On our way back to work we drive through McDonald's and I decide I should never question it again. I should accept it and enjoy it and be glad that, although I am not young enough to be part of this generation, whose questions about human sexuality were all answered by Internet porn, I am lucky enough to be tasting some of its fruit.

The Sleeper Has Awakened

I'm stopped at a red light on my way to work. I look over at the car next to me and see an average-looking woman using the rearview mirror to put her makeup on. I imagine her sucking my cock followed by me fucking her in several positions and finally blowing my load all over her freshly made-up face. This immediate reaction to a woman who is only averagely attractive is something I haven't experienced in a long time.

Once I get to work I stop in the coffee shop on the first floor to get a coffee and some gum. The girl who works the register, the same girl who has worked the register every morning for the past year or so, the girl who is probably in her late twenties, who is about five foot four and about two hundred pounds with a pierced eyebrow, hands me back my change and I can't help wondering what her pussy tastes like and wondering what her asshole looks like when you're fucking her doggy style and wondering if she gets many offers for no-strings-attached sex because she's so unattractive and wondering what her reaction would be to such an offer made by me. I take my coffee and gum and get in the elevator.

A woman gets in with me. She's unremarkable in every way: slightly older than me, average body, average face, bad perfume. I imagine biting her nipples and fingering her. I look down and can't see a panty line under the skirt she's wearing. I imagine fucking her hard against the wall of the elevator. She gets off on the next floor without making eye contact.

On my floor I pass several female coworkers, all of whom I see every day and none of whom has provoked any sexual thoughts since I've known them. I think about fucking them all in various positions, in various combinations, concluding with loads deposited in various locations on their respective persons.

I get to my desk and I'm almost ready to rape somebody in my office. This is the horniest I've been in a long fucking time. It's almost like I can taste every woman's pussy in the air as I pass her. I look out at Holly sitting at her desk. I look at her ass and accurately picture it naked sliding up and down on my dick.

At first I thought fucking Holly might just slake my thirst for sex. I thought it might actually make my relationship with my wife better. I thought it might quell my need to fuck, so that Alyna and I could exist in a more platonic relationship, which is clearly what she wants. But sitting at my desk, looking out at every woman in my office and imagining their pussies in my face as I eat them out—even Sandra Thomas, who is easily sixty-five years old and has a severe limp—I realize that fucking Holly has had the opposite effect.

Fucking Holly has awakened something in me that was asleep for a long time, for years. I am truly alive again.

chapter eighteen

The Thought Does Not Count

I get home from work, expecting to walk through the door and find Alyna watching TV with the kids followed shortly by a discussion about whether we have anything in the house for dinner or if I need to go pick something up. Instead, I open the door to find no Alyna and no kids. There's just a little note with my name on it lying on the rug just inside the front door.

It reads, "Kids are with Isabelle until 11. I'm in the bedroom." At one point during our therapy session, I remember, Roland told Alyna that she should be more spontaneous with sex, that it would potentially help both of us become more interested in having more of it. I assume this is her attempt at spontaneity. I get mildly excited by the idea of fucking my wife and then realize that, even after Alyna and I fuck, I will have fucked Holly more this month than I have my own wife. I push this out of my head and walk to the bedroom.

I open the door and see Alyna on the bed in lingerie, which I have no interest in, reading *A Walk Across the Sun*. She looks up and says, "Oh, I didn't hear you come in," then quickly reads a few more lines, marks her place with a bookmark, puts the book on the nightstand, and says, "Why don't you get out of those work clothes?"

I strip down in a few seconds and get in bed next to her. She says, "I bet you weren't expecting this today."

"No, I wasn't."

"Is it getting you excited?"

"Uh . . . yeah. You?"

"Sure. Yes."

She kisses me. It's a strange, forced kiss, almost vacant. It's almost what I would imagine a kiss with a prostitute to be like. I can easily tell that she's not into it, that she's doing it for some other reason. For Alyna, that reason is that it was ordered by her therapist. For a prostitute it would be money. The result is the same: a stiff, nonsexual kiss that seems unnecessary.

I stop her and roll her over on her back, take her lingerie off, and start kissing her down her stomach. It's obvious I'm making my way to her pussy. She says, "Wait. Let's just do it."

"Just fuck?"

"Yeah, just have sex. No foreplay."

"Why?"

"Just to be spontaneous."

Alyna clearly thought of the "no foreplay" scenario long before I got there, which of course makes it anything but spontaneous. I say, "Okay," and get a condom from the night table on my side of the bed. I say, "You want to put it on?" hoping this will play into her doctor-ordered sexual spontaneity.

She says, "No. You do it. You're better at it than I am."

I roll the thing down my dick and she says, "Let's do a position that we haven't done before."

I think back to when we first started dating, when we would fuck three times a day in every position in every hole. I think back to when she wanted to fuck. There isn't a position we haven't tried. I say, "I'm game. What did you have in mind?"

She says, "The pile driver."

I say, "What?"

"Yeah, it's like, I don't know. I looked it up online. It's like a porno thing. I thought you'd like it. It's like where the guy, you, kind of get up above me and squat down and I'm kind of like rolled back on my shoulders. Hang on, let me just show you."

I can feel my dick getting soft as she reaches over and gets her iPad. She cues up a video of a guy pile-driving some chick. I've seen the pile driver a million times. I just didn't know that's what it was called. It doesn't seem fun at all. It doesn't seem like it adds any sexual pleasure. It just seems like work.

I say, "Do you really want to do this, or is this something you think I want to do?"

She says, "I think it's something that we haven't done, and if we're trying to spice things up, we should do things that are new."

I say, "Alyna, you don't have to do this. I can tell you're not into it."

She says, "Yes, I am. I want us to have sex more. I know you think I'm fat now and I don't like sex, but it's not true. It's just that—" She starts crying. "We're just not the same people we were, you know? I want to want you to fuck me like we used to fuck before we were married, up against walls and in the shower and all of that, but it's just different for me somehow now. All I think about is the kids. I remember when all I thought about was your dick. That just seems like so long ago, and we can't be the same people we were then, right? I mean, we're parents now and that means things change, right? The things that were important to us before we had kids are different. That's all it means. I mean, is that terrible?"

She breaks down sobbing. I hug her and kiss her on the forehead. I say, "It's not terrible at all. Not at all."

Through tears she says, "I'm a good mom, right?"

I say, "You're a great mom. You really are," as my dick goes completely soft.

We lie there for another ten minutes. I console her about the state of our relationship. She assures me that she had only the best intentions when she set this whole thing up. I tell her that I appreciate the effort. She tells me she loves me and I tell her the same thing. Then I go to the bathroom and pull the unused condom off my limp dick.

chapter nineteen

Walking Dead

I'm sitting at a table with three other couples at the Woodland Hills Country Club having brunch. It's a pre-baby-shower being thrown by one of the couples for their closest friends. I am friends with none of these people. I know them only through casual exposure at other similar events that I've been forced to attend by Alyna, who actually is friends with these people. The real baby shower happens next weekend. We are obligated to bring gifts to both.

The women congratulate each other on every aspect of their lives in high-pitched laughter and praise. The men say little, chiming in only to confirm things their respective wives have said, and only if prompted to do so. Their default state is staring into space, or at each other, with the knowing dead-eyed gaze of a body and mind that no longer comprise a man. I used to think I was like them, but I can feel that I'm not anymore. I stare at a passing waitress's ass and I know that only very recently I had my dick in an ass that was younger and hotter. Only very recently I felt the mouth of a twenty-one-year-old girl on my dick. Only very recently I was reminded that we are all animals who exist only to eat and fuck.

Out of the corner of my eye, I see one of the other husbands, Craig I think his name is, catch me checking out our waitress's ass and probably gritting my teeth like a maniac. He looks at her ass, too, and raises his eyebrow nonchalantly, as if to say, "Wouldn't know what to do with it if I could get it."

I look at the other guys at the table. They're all like Craig. They're all resigned to their fate. They all understand that their lives are over except for the dying. They exist only to provide for their children, only to make sure their offspring will grow to reproduce their own offspring. I know I was like them before I fucked Holly. But I did fuck Holly, and I'm not like them anymore. Their lives have become slow trickles of meaningless moments spent watching children's television and listening to their wives fart in their sleep. They are no longer vital. I can't go back. I can't be like them again.

Gay Wisdom

I'm at lunch with Carlos. After I've filled him in on all the details of the affair I'm having with my twenty-one-year-old intern, he claps and says, "Finally, my straight married friend gets laid. Well, congratulations."

I say, "Thanks."

He says, "And you're doing okay with the guilt?"

I say, "Yeah, that's surprisingly easy to deal with. I just think about Alyna refusing to fuck, or not being into fucking anymore, and I can rationalize away the guilt pretty easily."

He says, "That's good. You have to get laid."

I say, "Actually the weirdest thing about all this is that I'll some-times question why this girl's fucking me at all, like what she finds attractive about me."

He says, "You're insecure? What a fucking pussy."

I say, "It's not insecurity. It's just questioning the whole thing, I guess. Does she really like me or not? You know?"

He says, "You're a pussy. But I'll break it down for you anyway. You said it yourself, when you told me she said she wanted a mature guy. You're mature. The guys she's used to don't have jobs, don't have money—"

I say, "Don't have a wife and kids."

He says, "You dumb fuck, that only makes you more attractive. Her little twenty-one-year-old girl brain doesn't know why that shit's attractive to her, but it is. She's biologically programmed to find it attractive. Her sole function as an organism on this planet is to find a guy to breed with who can provide for her offspring. Granted, the guys her age are hotter, in better shape, just more fucking virile all around—"

"Thanks."

"Well, they are. They can probably fuck better. Maybe not eat pussy better. You probably know better technique from experience. The point is, you've got something they don't: You've proven you can provide for a wife and kids, because you're fucking doing it. And deep down, under all of the layers of bullshit that I can only imagine you have to deal with when you fuck a girl that young, her inner self recognizes that you're a valuable biological choice. That's what she finds attractive about you. That's why she's fucking you."

"I guess that's not so bad."

"Not so bad? What did you think she was attracted to, how cool you are? The car you drive? Your fucking haircut?" He laughs.

"I don't know. Not how cool I am, I guess. Maybe something having to do with my personality and not just my marriage status."

"Yeah, I'm sure she can hang out with you and not want to hang herself, but trust me—you're not cool to her. You're old. You're interesting and you're more established than the guys she normally fucks. You should be happy about this shit. You're fucking a hot piece of twenty-one-year-old ass. That's a nice thing."

"Have you ever done anything like this?"

"Fuck a twenty-one-year-old?"

"Yeah."

"Uh . . . are you kidding? Tedward and I don't usually fuck anyone *over* twenty-one. So, yeah, I've done it. A lot."

"Okay, then."

"You don't have to be jealous. You just have to like dick and you could be doing it, too."

"And there's the trade-off."

The rest of the conversation is about nothing important, as our conversations usually are. Carlos tells me a little bit about his wedding and we get the check. When I get back to the office I look at Holly from my desk. I wonder if Carlos is right about why she fucks me—that I just represent a way to satisfy some primal urge that every girl has, that she has no actual interest in me as a person. She turns around and catches me looking at her. She smiles, turns back to her desk, and types something on her phone. My phone vibrates. I look down to see she has sent me a text message that reads, "Your hot." I overlook the spelling mistake and convince myself that Carlos is not entirely correct.

chapter twenty

Second Session

Roland says, "So did you guys try anything that I mentioned in the last session?"

Alyna says, "We did try something. But it didn't really work like I wanted it to, or like you said it would."

Roland says, "Okay. Can you elaborate a little bit?"

Alyna says, "Well, I planned a spontaneous, um, encounter, you know, and I even had a sexual position picked out that we'd never tried, and I dropped the kids off with a friend, but once we actually got close to having intercourse I just started thinking about the kids and about how I don't think I'm the same person I used to be and about how I don't know if that's a bad thing, it's just kind of how it is, and I'm not sure if having sex more or in weirder ways is going to change that for me, you know?" She's clearly trying to get the idea that we should be fucking more out of Roland's head.

Roland looks at me and says, "And how did you feel about all of this?"

I say, "I really did appreciate the effort. It just didn't work that time, and I guess I don't think it means we should give up on it or any-thing." I'm clearly trying to put the idea back into Roland's head that we should be fucking more.

Roland says, "Well, I think you should both be aware that these things, these changes, can't happen overnight. As long as you're both committed to making it work and to try and not give up, then you have nothing to worry about." That's my boy. I start wondering if there could be a market for a relationship therapist who always sides with the guys and always convinces women to fuck their partners more often and in more sexually adventurous manners. I wonder if I could become this therapist. I wonder what kind of schooling I would have to complete in order to get licensed. Roland is licensed, but he's certainly not a doctor. It can't be that tough. I make a mental note to remember this idea in case my other job goes belly-up at some point.

Roland says, "It's possible that the last suggestion I gave you was doing too much, too fast. Let's try something a little less involved. Tonight—"

Alyna says, "Tonight?"

Roland says, "Yes, tonight, I want you each to imagine it's the first time you're having sex."

I want him to get specific. I say, "With each other or the first time ever?"

He says, "Good question. With each other." Roland likes me. He says, "Try to remember what it was like when you first started dating, how you felt about each other physically, what it was like when you first began to feel each others' bodies. Really try to get back to that place in your heads."

Alyna says, "You want us to reenact the first time we had sex?"

Roland says, "No. Not at all. Don't think about the first time you had sex. I want you to pretend like tonight is the first time you two have ever had sex. For the rest of the day I want each of you to convince yourselves that you've never had sex, that you've been dating for a while but tonight is the night you're finally going to do it. Really try to work yourselves up for the rest of the day, and then tonight just cut loose."

Alyna says, "I can try to do that."

I say, "I can do that."

Roland says, "Good. This will be a good first step, I think, and it should be a little less pressure than what I suggested last time. I'd also like to make another suggestion to you."

I don't know what Roland is about to say, but I have full confidence that it will be heavily weighted in my favor based on the entirety of the therapy he's dispensed thus far. He says, "I think it's important in couples to reestablish some individuality if it feels like that's been lost. Couples should never be codependent or have an identity that is solely based on the couple as a unit. You should each be your own autonomous entities who are choosing to be together because it makes you better both together and on your own."

Alyna says, "So what are you saying? We should do things without each other?"

Roland says, "That's exactly what I'm saying. At least one night a week, maybe more, you should each go out with your friends separately or possibly just go out and do something alone. The point is to establish for yourselves that you have lives independent of one another, so that the time you do spend together isn't taken for granted. You might find that on these nights apart, you even miss each other a little bit, as crazy as that might sound."

Roland has basically given me carte blanche to fuck Holly whenever I want or to get drunk with Todd whenever I want. He is the greatest therapist in the world.

Roland spends the rest of the hour asking us about influences outside our relationship that might be contributing to our lack of sex. I talk about work. Alyna talks about the kids. I do not mention that I've been fucking my intern but look very forward to the next time I can do that, under the guise of taking some "me time."

chapter twenty-one

Burlesque Show

When I get home from work, I tell Alyna that I'm getting beers with Todd as part of my therapist-recommended individual identity-building time. She can't argue. Forty-five minutes later, I'm at a place Holly invited me to called Three Clubs, buying us both drinks and tickets to a backroom burlesque show featuring one of her friends.

Most of the chicks in the place are beasts. They're far more than just chubby and they're all dressed like Bettie Page. Holly is easily the hottest chick in the place. I'm glad to be with her. We sit down, engage in some meaningless small talk, and then the show starts.

I was under the impression that burlesque shows featured hot girls who were slightly too classy to actually work in a strip club but still like showing their tits to complete strangers and don't mind making one-tenth the money strippers do. Somehow no one ever explained to me that burlesque shows are actually endless parades of fat chicks with bad tattoos and hairdos from decades before their grandparents were born.

I don't make my disgust for these fat chicks known to Holly, because I know her friend is one of them. The announcer, a weird rockabilly Mexican guy with a wallet chain, takes the stage after five or six acts and says, "Are you ready for our final performer of the night?"

The fifty or so people in the audience all cheer. I refrain. He says, "Let's give a warm Three Clubs welcome to . . . Martini Blue!"

Holly says, "This is my friend." Everyone goes crazy. I'm expecting another fat chick to come out and flash her sloppy tits and cellulite, but instead the woman who comes through the curtain is one of the hottest girls I've ever seen. She has the standard incredibly pale and shittily tattooed look that all of the other burlesque dancers have had, but she's actually beautiful and she has an incredible body.

The first thing she does is rip off the little blue wig she's wearing and start twirling her black hair around. Then she does a routine that's similar to the ones all of the fat chicks before her have done and at the end she does the thing with her perfectly firm little B-cup tits where she makes the tassels spin in opposite directions. The announcer comes back out and thanks everyone for coming, and then the burlesque dancers start emerging from the behind the little makeshift stage where they all just performed. Holly says, "Let's get a drink with her."

At the bar I cover the tab for Holly and her friend. Her friend says, "Thanks."

I say, "No problem. Great show."

She says, "Thanks. Thanks for coming. I'm Cindy, by the way." We shake hands. She says, "So, how do you know Holly?"

Holly says, "We work together."

Cindy says, "Cool. You ever been to a burlesque show before?"

I say, "No, not really."

Cindy says, "Well, I hope your first experience was a good one."

We talk and drink for another hour. Most of the burlesque audience has cleared out and it's just Holly, Cindy, and me in a back corner, talking and drinking.

Cindy says, "So, I assume you guys are fucking, right?"

I look at Holly. I have no idea how to answer this question. I don't know what she's told her friends and I don't want to ruin any future chances I have of fucking her. I let her answer. She says, "Yeah, we fuck."

Cindy says, "Then what's up with that ring?" and points to my wedding ring.

I say, "Well, it means I'm married." This is the first time my marital status has been brought up in front of Holly. I hope this doesn't ruin things, and if it does, I silently vow to cave in Cindy's fucking skull with the heel of my shoe for bringing it up.

Cindy says to Holly, "And you're cool with that?"

Holly says, "Uh . . . yeah. Why wouldn't I be?"

Cindy says, "Cool with me if it's cool with you. That's probably pretty wild, though, right? I mean, fucking a hot younger girl? Is that like the craziest thing you've ever done?"

I say, "I don't know if it's the craziest."

Cindy says, "Then what's the craziest? Have you ever had a threesome?"

I say, "No, I haven't."

Cindy says, "Well, we both have."

My dick almost splits the table in half. I don't know exactly what's happening in this conversation, but it certainly seems like I'm about to be offered a threesome with Cindy and Holly. I try to play it cool. I say, "With each other or independently?"

Holly says, "With each other, but it was a while ago. Like last year with her ex-boyfriend."

I'm hoping Cindy feels some need to repay the favor Holly did for her ex-boyfriend. Cindy says, "It was seriously hot."

Still playing it cool, I say, "I bet."

Holly says, "Would you ever want to have a threesome?"

I can't tell if this is a trap or if she's really trying to find out if I'd fuck them both. I say, "Yeah, sure," and she grabs my leg under the table.

Holly says, "Well, what time is your curfew?"

I say, "I don't really have one."

Cindy says, "What about wifey?"

I say, "Not your concern."

Cindy says, "Oooh, he's like Don Draper."

Holly says, "I know."

I have never been compared to any actor, let alone a sex symbol of Jon Hamm's status. I decide this must have been what Carlos was talking about. They see me as something I'm not, merely because I'm older than them. I don't look this gift horse in the mouth. Trying to be smooth I say, "So where are we going next?"

Cindy takes out her phone and reads a text message or something, then says, "Oh shit, guys. My boyfriend got arrested. He got a DUI. I'm sorry, I have to make a call," and disappears.

I look at Holly and say, "That sucks."

She says, "I know. I was hoping we could have hooked that up."

I say, "Really? Was that really going to happen?"

She says, "Yeah. I think so." She takes a last sip of her drink, then looks me in the eye. "But don't worry. I'll make it up to you."

Half an hour later, I send Alyna a text telling her that I'm spending the night on Todd's couch. Holly and I go back to her dorm room, she kicks Carly out, and we sixty-nine for fifteen minutes or so with the lights on. I really get a chance to look at her asshole and her pussy. Her asshole is perfect. It's tiny and it's the same color as her skin. It has almost no convolutions. It's almost like she's a toy or something. Her pussy is even better. Tiny lips that aren't visible unless you spread it, and it tastes so fucking good I almost blow my load just from the idea of having it in my face. And the best part about the view I have of her pussy and asshole in the sixty-nine: there's no episiotomy scar. Eventually we fuck like wild animals for an hour. I'm on top of her, pressing her down into the bed with a hand on her chest, not letting her move, the full weight of my upper body holding her in place. I feel strong and in control, and she can tell, and it turns her on as much as it turns me on. She runs her fingers down the length of the forearm I'm using to pin her down, admiring it, feeling its weight against her chest. I fuck her harder and stare into her eyes.

She whimpers a little bit just before she cums, but never breaks our gaze. I'm full of this idea that I'm in control, that she's just there to make me cum, that I'm taking the thing I want most and she can't stop me. Just before I cum, I pull out, rip the rubber off, and jerk off all over her stomach and tits. She moans as I do this and says, "You're so fucking hot," then gets a towel from her closet and wipes my cum off herself. She get back in bed, and just before we pass out naked in her dorm-room single bed, forced to press our bodies intensely close together so we can both fit on the mattress, I say, "I fucking loved that view when we were sixty-nining."

She says, "What'd you like about it?"

I say, "You're perfect."

She says, "Thank you."

I wake up the next morning smelling like her pussy and more hungover than I've been in a long time. I borrow her toothbrush and take a shower in the dorm's community shower. It should be stranger than it is to me. I actually find it kind of fun, like I'm young again.

We drive to work in separate cars.

Father's Son

I'm sitting in my chair watching Andy play *Mario Kart* on Wii. Every once in a while he'll say, "Look, Daddy," before he uses a power or knocks another racer off a track. My hand is near my face and I can still smell Holly's pussy on my fingers. It's faint but it's there.

I wonder if Andy will ever be like me. I wonder if he'll ever cheat on his wife with a younger woman. I wonder if he'll have kids who won't know he's fucking a woman who's not their mother. I wonder if he'll be gay. If he is, I hope he turns out like Carlos, who always seems happy to be gay.

I wonder what Andy's first girlfriend will be like. It's not that long until he'll be taking some girl to prom and trying to fuck her that night. It's not that long until he starts to see women the way I do. It's not that long until he breaks a girl's heart and has his heart broken and ends up stuck with someone who has changed so drastically that he doesn't even want to fuck her anymore. I pity him for the life ahead of him, and I hope that he can avoid these things, but I know that will be virtually impossible.

He says, "Look, Daddy," and I say, "I am, bud, I am looking."

chapter twenty-two

Amateur Porn

Sometimes we let the kids stay up a little past their normal bedtime and watch TV with us. I'm in my chair with Jane in my lap. Alyna and Andy are on the couch and we're watching *American Idol*, which only Alyna gives a shit about. We're at the point in the season when the only real hot chick they had on the show has been voted off, and it's down to a few closeted gay guys and a brain-dead country bumpkin who always sings about Jesus and America. I'm sure he'll win for these reasons.

I look over at Alyna and Andy. He's sitting in her lap and she's stroking his hair. He's absolutely soothed. There's no place in the world he'd rather be than right there in his mom's lap in this moment. She's a good fucking mom, and I realize that maybe the cost of having a good mom for your kids is losing the person you loved, losing the person you fucked, losing the person who still wants to fuck you. I wonder if it's just a phase for her. I wonder if, when the kids get older, she won't revert to her old self again. I think of the girl I used to think about when I jerked off, and I wonder if I'll ever get her back.

My phone buzzes in my pocket. I take it out and see that I have a new message from Holly. I'm reluctant to open it while every member of my family is sitting within ten feet of me, but the little shot of adrenaline I get every time I see she's sent me a text message is too much to deny and I open it. It's a picture of her ass and pussy, basically a POV shot as though the camera is my face and she's sitting on it. The accompanying text reads, "I hope you like the picture as much as the real thing."

I quickly look over at Alyna to make sure she's not watching me. She's not. Jane still seems too young to know what the fuck is going on with anything, and she didn't see it anyway.

I bring the phone up close to my face so I can really study the photo. It's even more perfect than I remember, and all I can think about is when I can have it in my face again. I imagine that this feeling I have, this all-consuming, burning desire to fuck her again, to bury my face in her pussy again, to just feel her again, is similar to what a heroin addict must feel.

I text her back a message that reads, "I could never like anything more than the real thing, but keep sending me pictures. This is so hot."

Over the course of the final fifteen minutes of *American Idol*, Holly sends me a picture of her fingering herself, a picture of her fingering her asshole, a picture of her tits, a picture of her sliding the back end of a toothbrush up her asshole while she fingers her pussy, a picture of her watching porn on her computer and fingering herself, and eventually a picture of her fingers glistening with pussy juice and a text that reads, "I came thinking about you fucking me in the ass. More when I get horny again."

I turn my phone's screen off and set it on the ground next to my chair. Then, in a moment of paranoia I think it's actually a better idea to slide the phone under my chair as I wonder if it's completely deplorable that I just thought about fucking a twenty-one-year-old girl in every hole while my two-year-old daughter was sitting in my lap. I rationalize that it's probably happened a million times and it's not that big a deal unless Jane were ever to find out, which she won't, so fuck it. Doesn't matter.

chapter twenty-three

Mistakes Were Made

I'm in my office staring at Holly when she gets up from her desk and walks into my office with a pouty look on her face. She says, "I've been texting you all day and you haven't texted me back. I even went to the bathroom and sent you some, you know, naughty stuff."

I say, "Fuck. I left my phone at home." I had searched for it this morning before giving up, but only now do I realize that it's still under the chair in my living room where I left it last night. I say, "I'll look at them when I get home, though. I'm looking forward to that."

Holly says, "When's the next time we can hang out?"

I say, "I don't know. Probably next week I can get away for a night."

She walks over close to me and leans in and whispers in my ear, "I want your fucking cock in my ass again," then licks my ear and walks out. I look over through my window to see Dan Persons staring at me from his desk. The surprised look on his face betrays the fact that he must have seen the entire exchange between me and Holly. I'm sure I'm caught. This is bad on several levels. I imagine a scenario in which Dan tells Lonnie that I'm fucking the intern,

Lonnie fires me, and then I have to go home and tell Alyna I got fired, and when she asks me why, I'll have to come up with some story about the economy and cutbacks and hope the real story never gets back to her. Then Dan smiles at me and gives me a thumbs-up. Everything's fine.

I get through the rest of the day and head home. When I get there, Alyna answers the door crying.

I say, "What's wrong?"

She holds up my phone with a picture of Holly's ass on it along with a text that reads, "Your cock needs to be in this."

Alyna says, "What in the fuck is this?"

My brain is fucked. It's like pouring water on a computer. Nothing works right. I can't get to the second step of any thought. First words of potential sentences I could say next keep replacing themselves in my head. Roland flashes through my cycle of stuttering thoughts for a brief second. Roland could get out of this situation. He'd have some fucking incredible thing to say that would calm Alyna down and make her realize that this is a necessary part of building an individual identity. But I'm not Roland. I say, "Is that my phone?"

Alyna says, "Uh . . . *yes* it's your fucking phone, asshole. It was buzzing under your chair every five minutes."

I say, "How'd you get my password?"

Alyna says, "Your password for everything is your birthday, you dipshit."

That's a mistake I'll never make again. If this is going to happen, I don't want the kids to be around. I say, "Where are the kids?"

Alyna says, "Fuck you. They're with Isabelle. You think I want them in the same house with you, you disgusting fucking pig?"

I say, "Just calm down. What are you talking about? That thing is just a joke from one of the guys at work." It's a terrible lie, but the best one I can come up with as I can feel the blood draining from my face and my heart beating in my asshole.

Alyna says, "Really?"

I say, "Yeah, they text around pictures of naked chicks from the Internet. It's like a little interoffice guy thing."

Alyna says, "That's some joke, because whatever guy from work this is has really been sending you a lot of these texts, and not just today but for the past few weeks. And look at this one." She scrolls through Holly's texts until she comes to one of my responses. "You even replied to a few of them. 'I want you to suck my cock and then ride it until you cum on it.' That's a pretty funny joke. He must have laughed his ass off when he got this one."

I take the phone out of her hand so she can't wield it like a murder weapon at a trial and say, "Alyna, it's just text messages. It's nothing."

Alyna says, "Shut up. Just shut up and stop lying. I've read every text message you've sent to this person. I know that when you said you were at Todd's, you were with her. You were . . . fucking her. How could you do this?"

This is immediately recognizable as the worst moment in my life even as it's happening. I don't regret fucking Holly, but I never wanted Alyna to have to go through any of what's happening right now. Even if there were ever a time when I would have wanted her to know about Holly, I wouldn't have wanted her to find out like this. She's sobbing and angry, and more than that, she's hurt. She's devastated. I've ripped out the heart of the woman who is the mother of my children and I'm watching her bleed in front of me.

It tears me apart to see Alyna like this. She might not want to fuck me, but in that moment I know that I love her as much as I ever have and I hate the fact that I've caused her this much pain. Her face and her tears are enough for me to say, "Alyna, I'm so sorry. I didn't . . . it was just a stupid thing to do. I love you and I . . . It's over between me and her. I mean, it was never really anything anyway, but it's done."

I move in to hug her as she sobs. She steps back from me and says, "Get the fuck out of this house."

I say, "Alyna, come on. Let's talk about this."

Alyna says, "No. There's nothing to talk about here. You're a fuck-ing piece of shit and you can't sleep under the same roof as me and the kids. Not tonight. I'll give you five minutes to pack some shit and get out."

I look at her. She won't look back at me. She just leans against the wall sobbing. There's no way I'm talking myself back into the house tonight.

I go upstairs and throw some shit in a Lakers duffel bag that I use to carry my gym shit. I get a few work shirts, some pants, underwear, socks, whatever my numb brain can conjure up. This is the worst I have ever felt in my life. I have potentially destroyed my family. Holly is the best piece of ass I've ever had, but still, it doesn't seem worth this.

I think back to what Todd said about his dad and Maria Reynaldi. It's easy to look back from your deathbed and regret the girls you didn't fuck when you had the chance. But what if he had fucked her and it had ripped his family apart? Would he even remember what it was like to have fucked her? Or would he just remember the look on his wife's face when she found out?

I convince myself that there's a chance to make things right here and to repair what I've done. I convince myself that Alyna just needs some time away from me, and then a heartfelt apology, and that doing everything she asks of me, including more therapy sessions, will get me back in the house. As uncertain as I am about everything in the immedi-ate future, I am certain that Roland will no longer be on my side, but I'm prepared to eat as much shit as necessary in order to fix this.

I toss my toothbrush in the bag and head back to the front door, where Alyna is still crying. I say, "Okay, I'm leaving. But I want to talk to you when you're ready, okay?"

Alyna says, "I don't know."

I say, "I love you."

Alyna says, "Just go."

I say, "Tell the kids I love them," and she breaks down, sobbing uncontrollably. I want to hug her, to make even the smallest piece of this whole thing be slightly less shitty for her, but I can't. I just walk back out to my car and start it. I can't feel anything except the air conditioner blowing on my face as I drive to the Warner Center Marriott in a daze.

chapter twenty-four

First Night

My room is shitty and small. I have no idea how long I'll be staying here, but I refuse to take my clothes out of my duffel bag and put them in drawers or in the closet or anything like that. I lay down on the bed and turn on the TV so there's some noise, something to take my mind off what just happened, off what's still happening. I watch TV for a few minutes. It doesn't work. I'm stuck in some weird kind of emotional shell-shock that doesn't seem to be going away or resolving into any real emotion.

I take my phone out and look at all of the text messages Holly sent me over the course of the day. There are two pictures, one of her ass and one of her tits, and several sexually suggestive text messages. Alyna read them all. She read them all and I know she probably read every other text message that's ever been in my phone. Holly's are the only ones that matter, the only ones that aren't meaningless conversations between me and Todd or me and Alyna. If I had just remembered my phone none of this shit would be happening. I'd be back at home watching the *American Idol* results show and wondering when I'd be able to fuck Holly next.

It dawns on me that now I can fuck Holly anytime I want. This line of thought gives me something other than numbness. I go with it. I text her the following message: "Want to hang out tonight?" I spend the next few minutes looking back over all of the naked pictures she's sent me until she replies with a text that reads, "Can't tonight. Plans." I wonder what her plans are. What plans could a twenty-one-year-old girl have? I'm sure they involve alcohol and drugs and not wondering if her husband is going to divorce her and not wondering how her children will react to her not sleeping under the same roof as them for the first time in their lives.

Realizing I will be alone in this room without being bothered by anyone, I unzip my pants and start jerking off. It doesn't work. I don't even get hard because I can't stop thinking about my kids and about Alyna crying and about what she must be telling them about me and about how this is all going to end.

I go to the bar downstairs and drink by myself for a few hours. *American Idol* is on the TV. One of the closeted gay guys gets kicked off. I pay my tab and head back upstairs, where I take a long shower and get into bed.

It's the first time in a long time that I've slept in a bed alone. I miss the noises of my house. The ticking of the refrigerator, the low hum of the air conditioner, the slight crackle of the baby monitor that we still keep in the kids' room. I close my eyes and I miss all of the shit that annoyed me about sleeping with Alyna. I miss the way she would put her cold feet on my legs to warm them, I miss the way she would exhale so hard through her nose as she slept that it would feel like she was poking me with an index finger, I miss the way she would twitch slightly when she would fall asleep, I miss the way her hair would get in my face when she'd force me to spoon her. I miss the way her aging, out-of-shape body felt against my aging, out-of-shape body. I miss my wife.

Repairs

My cell phone freezes. I take the battery out and restart it. It works for a second, but when I open the text application it freezes again. I do this five more times and get the same result each time. I stop at a Sprint store on my way to work and speak with Gus, a customer service representative who obviously hates his job and everyone on planet Earth.

He says, "What's the problem?" in a tone that makes me think he'll probably kill himself by the end of the day.

I say, "Every time I try to read or send a text, the phone freezes."

He says, "Did you try taking the battery out and restarting it?"

I say, "Several times."

He takes the battery out and restarts it. He opens the text application and it freezes. He says, "Yeah, that didn't work. So we'll just reset it. That should fix the problem."

"Won't that erase everything I have on the phone?"

"Your contacts are saved to your Google account."

"Right, but all of my text messages, my pictures, all of that's gone if you reset it, right?"

"Did you save that stuff to the phone or to the memory card?"

"Some is saved to the phone and some to the memory card. Can you just back up everything and put it all back on the phone after the reset to be sure I get everything?"

"It takes a little more time, but I guess."

"Okay, thanks."

I wait while Gus goes into a back room and backs up everything on my phone. I'm positive this process will involve him getting to look at every photo Holly sent me of her ass and tits, as well as every filthy text message she sent me explaining what she was going to do to my cock. I'm also positive that Gus and all of the other assholes who work here see so much of this shit every day that it probably doesn't faze them in the least. Unless they come across something extremely out of the ordinary, like a picture of a guy with a peanut butter jar up his ass or something, they probably don't even take the time to show the other guys in the back room. I imagine a wall of pictures they've printed out that are kind of a hall of fame of the weirdest shit they've ever seen on customers' phones. I convince myself that this photo hall of fame must exist in every cell-phone store in America.

I watch a woman with a baby in a stroller looking at phones while she's waiting for hers to be fixed. She's not attractive. I think about fucking her and blowing my load on her ample tits. I imagine a scenario in which she's actually here to get her husband's phone fixed and Gus and the guys in the back see all of the naked pictures of all of the chicks that her husband is cheating on her with but they don't tell her. I wonder how many times that happens. I wonder how many times the wife does find out about her husband cheating through some discovery of a text message or Facebook post. I can't decide if we're better off or worse. It seems like all of this shit makes it much easier to fuck chicks, but it makes it much harder to keep any of it a secret.

chapter twenty-five

The Meet

Alyna left a message on my newly repaired cell phone that said, "Meet me at the Baker for lunch tomorrow. 1 P.M. Don't be late." She didn't actually call me. She just recorded and sent the message to meet her at her favorite café. I imagine three scenarios as I drive to the Baker.

I imagine her showing up with divorce papers and demanding that I sign them or never see my kids again. I imagine her telling me that she forgives me and she'll take me back as long as I never talk to Holly again, which I don't know if I'm prepared to do just yet. And I imagine her not showing up at all but, instead, a hired killer who slits my throat and pisses on my corpse. I realize the first two scenarios are much more likely, but still, the third is possible.

When I walk in she's already there. She doesn't smile. She doesn't even get out of her chair. She just looks at me. She doesn't seem angry or even upset. She just seems to be there. I sit down and I say, "Hey."

She says, "Hey."

I say, "So, what's . . . I mean . . . I don't know what to say here, really. Do you want to know where I'm staying?"

Alyna says, "I don't give a fuck where you're staying."

I say, "Okay. How are the kids? What'd you tell them?"

She says, "I told them there was something extremely important at work and you might have to be gone for a little while."

This gives me some hope that she sees a possible reconciliation. I reason that she would have outright told the kids I was a cheating pile of shit, or maybe told them that I died, or something far more final than that I might have to be gone for a little while, if she thought there was no chance of ever repairing things between us. I say, "Okay. So why did you want to meet?"

She takes a deep breath and says, "I guess I just . . . in that moment when I found your phone, I obviously couldn't think straight. I saw Roland and he said that I should at least hear your side of the story. Whether I believe anything you say at this point is up in the air, but he said I should at least hear you out. He said that I owed it to you and to me to listen."

Roland continues to impress me. I say, "Okay. Well, what do you want to know?"

She says, "Everything, I guess. I read the texts. I know you've been fucking this girl." She's starting to get pissed again. "And I do mean *girl*. What is she, eighteen? Is she *even* eighteen? Are you a fucking statutory rapist on top of being a cheating piece of shit?"

I don't want to say any of the shit I'm about to say, but I figure at this point lying will only make everything that happens in the next few months worse than it has to be. It seems to me that all of the lies will get uncovered anyway, so I say, "She's twenty-one. She's an intern at my office. It hasn't been going on that long."

Alyna says, "And what do you see in her? I mean, why her?"

I want to say that it's because she's hot as fuck and her ass is as tight as a trampoline, but I just say, "Honestly, she paid attention to me. That was it."

Alyna says, "And I don't?"

I say, "No. Not anymore."

Alyna says, "Don't you fucking turn this around and try to make it about how I neglected poor little you."

I say, "I'm not. You asked me 'Why her?' That's why."

Alyna says, "We have two fucking children. How could you do this to them?"

This one hurts a little more than I expected. I say, "I don't know. It just happened."

Alyna says, "But then it happened again and again, right?"

I say, "Yeah."

Alyna says, "Not that I'd be any better with it just happening one time, but I'd at least understand that more. This is . . . seriously, are you planning on dating this girl, this fucking child?"

I say, "No. Come on."

Alyna says, "Well, what am I supposed to think?"

I say, "I don't know," and I realize that I don't even really know the answer to her question. I haven't thought of the possibility of dating Holly, of trying to have something more with her than fucking and flirting at the office, until this moment, until my wife brought it up. For a fleeting second, I can see us together. It doesn't seem that strange to me. But then I imagine getting to see Andy and Jane only every other weekend, and being the dad who was never around for them. I say, "I guess you're supposed to think that I fucked up."

Alyna says, "No shit."

I say, "And that I'm an asshole."

Alyna says, "No shit."

I say, "And that I'm still the father of our children and that I still love them and you very much. I just made a mistake."

Alyna says, "Is that an apology?"

I say, "Well, yeah."

Alyna says, "Well, it's not accepted. You didn't just make a mistake. You're having an affair."

I say, "Come on. It's not an affair."

Alyna says, "You're fucking the same girl multiple times outside of your marriage. That's the definition of an affair, you stupid fucking asshole." In this moment I start to wonder why she wanted to do this in a public place. Maybe she thought it would keep her from crying, but I think her unbridled anger is serving that function. She says, "There was a time when I would have done anything for you, when I trusted you beyond anyone I ever thought I could trust. We had something really good."

I say, "Then why—"

Alyna says, "Shut up. We had something really good. And you fucking ruined it. How can I ever trust you again? If you thought we weren't having enough sex before this, how did you think this would make it better? Now, when I look at you, all I see are those pictures that girl sent you. How am I supposed to get over that, to move on from that?"

I say, "I don't know."

Alyna says, "Neither do I. I really just wanted to see you today to see if I could find anything in myself that's able to forgive this. And I'm not saying I can't find it, but I can't find it right now."

I say, "I understand."

Alyna says, "No, you don't. I've thought a lot about this, about us, about what we were like when we were younger, when we first met, how good everything was, and I know things have changed. But they never changed so much for me that I needed to fuck somebody else. I'm here right now for the kids, and anything that happens between us after this is because of them."

I say, "Okay," and we sit there in silence for a few seconds.

Alyna eventually says, "Where are you staying?"

The Thing I Miss Most

I haven't talked to Alyna in a few days. I don't really know what's going to happen with us, but I've decided to fuck Holly as many times as I can until something does happen to resolve things with Alyna. Holly told me she likes fucking in a hotel room because it makes her feel dirty. I see no reason to waste this opportunity.

Holly comes over and we fuck for an hour or so, then get room service and watch some TV before passing out. I wake up in the middle of the night and Holly's asleep next to me in my bed. I look over at her. She's rolled to the other side of the bed and turned away from me, curled up in a little ball, lightly snoring. That's how she sleeps. She can fuck, but she clearly has issues with affection and any kind of physical intimacy that isn't X-rated. I wonder if it's just her or if it's generational. I miss having someone to sleep with who actually sleeps with me, sleeps next to me, actually shares the experience of sleeping instead of just being unconscious in the same bed. I start thinking about Alyna, specifically about her fat ass, and get surprisingly horny. I think about waking up Holly for a second round of fucking, but I don't.

Instead I creep out of bed, get my laptop, and sneak into the bathroom. I bring up NudeVista.com on the hotel Wi-Fi and search "fat ass POV." Most of the results are actually chicks with giant fat asses, cellulite everywhere. These women are beasts. But on the second page of results near the bottom is a beautiful brunette with the exact kind of ass I was looking for. It's just like Alyna's, the same exact shape, but younger and with less cellulite. This girl's name is Brooke Lee Adams. I make a mental note of it and then jerk off to a video of her getting fucked doggy-style. If I concentrate hard enough, I can remember fucking Alyna doggy-style when her ass looked more like Brooke Lee Adams's than it does now.

I cum into the toilet, flush, wipe off a glob of semen that didn't go down with a wad of toilet paper, flush again, make sure it goes down so that Holly doesn't see it when she gets up to take a piss, shut my computer down, and slide back into bed wondering if I'll ever fuck Alyna again.

chapter twenty-six

Snip

I had kind of forgotten about my vasectomy due to the complete fucking nightmare I've been living for the past week where my marriage is concerned. So when the urologist's office calls to confirm my appointment, I initially think it's pointless to go through with it, and I tell them I have to cancel. But after a few minutes of staring at Holly's ass as she sits in the chair outside my office, and wondering what it would feel like to fuck her without a rubber, I call them back to cancel my initial cancellation.

I opt for the non-scalpel vasectomy. My doctor and the urologist he recommended both seem to think it's the best option, the quickest healing and the least painful.

I'm sitting in the urologist's office after filling out my paperwork when a nurse comes out and says, "Okay, we're all ready for you." I stand up and take my last steps as a fully functioning reproductive male.

In the doctor's office, the nurse tells me to take off my clothes and put on a surgical gown. Then she tells me to sit on the table and gets out a little sponge, a razor, and some kind of disinfecting solution. She then proceeds to clean and shave the front of my ball bag. No other part, just the front of my ball bag. I imagine her sucking my dick while she's down there. I wonder if she has some sexual fetish that can only be satisfied by swallowing guys' last loads that contain sperm. After she finishes shaving the front of my ball bag she says, "Okay, looks good. The doctor will be in in a minute," then she leaves. She does not suck my dick.

I lift my surgical gown and look at her handiwork. I've never actually seen my balls without hair on them. I've shaved my ball hairs down before, but always just a trim, never down to the skin this way. It looks weird. My ball bag is shriveled and loose. It looks like chewed bubble gum. I try to remember the last time I really inspected my balls or dick. I can't.

The door opens and the nurse comes back in with the urologist. They catch me looking at my balls. The urologist says, "Saying your good-byes? Just kidding. I'm Dr. Klein. It's nice to meet you. I think we can have you out of here in about half an hour."

I say, "Sounds good."

He says, "Just lie back on the table," and I do. Then he goes over to the counter and puts on some rubber gloves. I've never had a dude handle my dick or balls for more than just a routine hernia check. This seems like it will require more intimacy. I wonder if he's ever had a guy get a hard-on while he was cutting on their ball bag. I assume this will not happen to me.

He comes over to the table I'm lying on and says, "Everyone approaches this differently, and I want to make this as comfortable as possible for you. So would you like warnings as I'm about to do things, or would you like me to just do it as quickly as possible?"

I say, "I'd actually like you do it as accurately as possible, if that's an option."

He laughs and says, "Yes, of course."

I say, "And I guess I'd like warnings."

He says, "Okay, here's your first one. You're going to feel a little pinch," then he jabs a needle into my fucking ball bag. It's surprisingly not that painful. I've had tetanus shots that were worse. After a few seconds he starts fucking around with my nuts, but they're numb. Whatever he's doing gives me only a general idea that he's doing anything at all. He says, "Can you feel that?"

I say, "I don't think so."

He says, "Okay, I think we're ready." I start to get a little nauseated.

The nurse hands him a little instrument that looks almost like a screwdriver. He goes back to work in my crotch. He says, "You might feel a little pressure now." I can feel a vague pulling on my ball bag and then a pop, like a hole being punched in rubber. He says, "Okay, step one all done. You okay?"

I say, "Yeah."

He hands the screwdriver thing back to the nurse and she hands him another screwdriver-looking thing with what I think is a curved hook at the end. This thing looks medieval. This is a thing you do not want near your fucking balls. He goes back into my crotch with it and says, "Okay, now you might feel a little pulling sensation," and that's exactly what I feel. It feels like he's pulling one of my nuts out through the hole he poked in my ball bag. I know this isn't the case, but that's what it fucking feels like. I start to get a little more queasy just thinking about it. Then he hands the hook thing back to the nurse and she gives him this little wand-looking thing.

He says, "Almost done with the first one," then moves the wand thing close to my ball bag and for a brief second I smell burning flesh. I think he just cauterized the tube that goes from my balls to my dick. I'm getting a little more nauseated. He says, "Okay, one down," then hands the wand thing back to the nurse and gets the hook thing from her again. By the time he finishes the same thing on the other nut, and puts a little Band-Aid on the hole he made in my nut sack, I'm almost positive I'm going to puke. But then it's over and I power through my last few minutes on the table with the front of my ball bag shaved and both my nuts separated from my dick.

Dr. Klein says, "Easy enough, right?"

I say, "I guess so."

He says, "Okay. I'm going to prescribe you something for the pain, if you should have any, and you should stay off your feet for the next few days if you can."

I say, "Oh, I thought I could go back to work."

He says, "Look, honestly, you're pretty young. You'll be fine. Just try to keep your feet elevated, so we don't get any hematomas or anything. Believe me, you don't want to see that. And call me if you notice any pain that might be abnormal." I wonder what kind of pain would be considered normal where having your balls separated from your dick is concerned.

He says, "And you should lay off any sexual activity for the next week or so and continue to use condoms for the next month or so until we can get you back in here to collect a semen sample and make sure you're firing blanks."

I say, "All right."

He says, "Do you have someone giving you a ride home?"

I say, "No, should I?"

He says, "Did we not recommend that you have a ride?"

I say, "You did, but I don't really have one. Is that terrible?"

He says, "Again, you'll probably be fine. Just ice it if there's any swelling and wear tight briefs for the next week or so."

I say, "Okay."

He writes something in my file and hands it to the nurse, then says, "Well, that's all I've got. Do you have any other questions?"

I say, "No. I don't think so."

He says, "Okay. It was nice meeting you. And, again, call me if there are any complications, but I think it went perfectly." Then he leaves.

The nurse says, "Okay, get dressed and meet me out front when you're ready. Take your time."

I get up off the table and look at the Band-Aid on my shaved ball bag. It's strange. I know it's not true, but I picture my balls free-floating in my scrotum, attached to nothing in my body, having no actual purpose anymore. I put on my clothes, walk out front, schedule a time to come in and jerk off to have my semen analyzed, then drop off my pain-med prescription on my way back to work.

In my office I put my feet up on my desk and look at Holly. I imagine fucking her without a rubber. And then I realize that, without the ability to even jerk off, the next week is going to be a living hell.

chapter twenty-seven

Demands Are Made

Alyna has invited me back to my own house for dinner. I'm looking forward to seeing the kids, but when I show up they're not home. Alyna says she left them with Isabelle for the night. I know it seems highly unlikely, but some part of me hopes she's going to initiate some crazy night of sex in order to win me back by proving to me that I don't need to be fucking people outside the relationship, that she's somehow trans-formed herself back into the insatiable woman she was when we met.

She says, "I made chicken. I hope that's okay." She's being extremely civil. It's clearly forced. I don't know what the fuck's going on. It feels like she's purposely trying to trick me into letting my guard down, and then she's going to have some guy come out and club me on the head or something.

I say, "Yeah. I like your chicken."

We walk into my dining room, which we used maybe once or twice before all of this shit happened. The table is set with the good plates, which we also only used once or twice before all this shit went down. I'm starting to think that maybe my raunchy fuckfest idea was dead on the money. I wonder if she'll let me fuck her in the ass. The only pussy I've gotten for a while now has been Holly's, and although she's clearly in better shape than Alyna, the allure of something different is always strong. My wife has become the something different. I imagine sliding my dick into her asshole and squeezing her fat ass. It appeals to me more than I ever thought it would.

Then I realize that I've totally forgotten about my vasectomy. It's only been six days. I decide that, if the shit starts going down, I'll throw caution to the wind. I haven't had any abnormal pain since the operation. Like Dr. Klein said, I'm young enough. I should be fine.

I sit down at one end of the dining room table and Alyna pours some wine for us both. We're definitely fucking. She only drinks wine when she wants to fuck. We take our glasses and she raises hers and says, "Cheers."

I say, "To what?"

She says, "Uh . . . how about to figuring things out?"

I was hoping for something more along the lines of "To showing you I can still be the filthy cock-whore you married five years ago," but at least it's a step toward that possibility. I say, "Cheers to figuring things out."

We take a sip and she says, "Let me get dinner."

She brings out two salads and two plates of chicken and vegetables. Before I take the first bite, a brief and insane thought flashes through my mind that she might be poisoning me. I wonder if I should tell her my fork is dirty and ask her to get me another one, and then switch our plates when she goes back into the kitchen. She cuts a piece of chicken. It's too late. She'd notice the whole chicken on her plate if I switched them. Fuck it. I take a bite. Tastes fine.

She says, "So, thanks for coming over."

I say, "Thanks for having me." It's weird. This forced politeness in my own fucking house is starting to get to me. I want to cut through the shit and just ask her why she invited me over, but I don't want to ruin whatever she's got going on in case it is the fuckfest.

We talk about innocuous shit—my job, how the kids are doing, fucking *American Idol*—as we polish off the first bottle of wine. I can tell she's a little buzzed, and this only strengthens my theory that she wants to get fucked tonight, that she's seen the error of her ways and maybe she hasn't forgiven me for anything that's happened but she recognizes her role in why it happened.

She says, "Should I open another bottle?"

I say, "I'm game."

She gets another bottle and pours us two more glasses. She takes a big sip and says, "Okay, I think I'm drunk enough to do this now." I can feel my dick starting to get a little hard at the prospect of fucking my wife again. I wonder if she shaved for tonight. I'm hoping she has if she's planning on us fucking. She says, "So, the reason I asked you over here tonight is . . ."

I'm ready for her to stand up, turn around, and hike her skirt up so I can see her ass or something equally enticing. Maybe she'll tell me she missed the taste of my cock or just needed to be fucked again.

She says, " . . . I have some demands."

This is not exactly what I was expecting, but I'm still thinking maybe they'll be filthy demands. Maybe she'll demand that I fuck her in the ass and cum on her face.

She says, "I have some demands, and I think that's okay given the situation. And I think the only way this is going to work is if you meet all of them." It's sounding less and less like fucking to me.

She takes out a little piece of paper and unfolds it. She says, "I wrote these down so I could just go through them and not forget any and so I could get it all out, so just listen."

This is definitely not about sex in any way. This is the worst dinner in my own home that I've ever had in my life.

She says, "Demand number one. You cannot have any contact with this girl ever again."

I say, "I work with her."

Alyna says, "Shut up. Demand number two. You can drive to and from work. That's it. All other times you have to be here, at home, with us. If you want to hang out with Todd and have beers or something, he has to come here." She looks at me, waiting for a protest that I don't offer. She continues, "Demand number three. I will have full access to your cell phone and your Facebook and whatever else you use to talk to anyone that's not me. Demand number four. You will have exactly one minute to respond to any text message or phone call that you receive from me. If you don't respond within the minute, I'll assume you're cheating on me and this is all over. And the last one—demand number five. You will not even think about asking me for sex until I tell you I'm ready again."

I say, "What did Roland say about all of this?"

She says, "He doesn't know. I stopped going to Roland because he didn't really help all that much, in case you haven't noticed. So . . ."

I say, "So what?"

She says, "So what do you think? Can you do this? Can you make this right and do what I need you to do here?" I have no idea what to say. I'm a fucking deer in the headlights. There's no way it's even possible for any human being to meet those demands. But I know I want to live in my house again. I want to see my kids again. I think I want my wife back again. At least I want my old wife back again, the one who used to fuck me. But after this I don't even know if that's ever going to be possible. I say, "Why'd you have the kids stay with Isabelle?"

She says, "Because I wanted us to be able to talk about this without interruption and without the kids influencing any of this."

I say, "But they do influence it. How can they not?"

She says, "Okay, well then, how are they influencing it? What's your decision?"

I say, "Do I have to have one right now? This is a lot to take in."

She says, "If you don't want to make this right badly enough to know the answer now, immediately, then you don't want to make it right."

I say, "Alyna, that's not it. This is just a lot to deal with. And some of those demands don't even seem remotely possible to meet."

She says, "Which ones?"

I say, "Like the one about texting you back within a minute. What if I'm in a meeting or something, or I leave my phone in my office when I go to lunch?"

She loses her forced politeness and she loses the rest of her composure, too. She starts crying. "You just want to fuck that little whore some more, don't you? And then, once you think you've gotten it all out of your system, you'll come crawling back. Well, that's not how it works. I'm willing to extend this olive branch right now. You take it or it disappears. That's it."

I say, "Alyna, can I have a day to process this?" That sounds like something Roland would say.

She says, "Get the fuck out. I knew this was a stupid idea. You're an asshole and you ruined our family. Get the fuck out of this house."

I don't argue. I don't take another bite of food or another sip of wine. I stand up and walk out the front door. She doesn't follow me so I lock the door to my own house behind me.

First Load

I wake up with a hard-on that feels like a roll of quarters. Per my doctor's orders I haven't jerked off in six days. This is day seven. I don't know if I'm supposed to wait until day eight to blow a load or if the week officially ends on day seven. I decide to take a chance. Before I even get out of bed or take a piss, I start going to town.

I'm on my back, imagining that Holly is straddling me with my cock in her ass. It only takes me a minute or so of solid jerking until I can tell I'm about to blow my load. So far nothing feels strange or painful, but I still have a general unease about what might happen next. I slow my stroke for a second, unable to help thinking about my balls exploding in my scrotum and ejaculating blood. I'm reminded of the scene in *Antichrist* when Willem Dafoe gets his cock smashed while he's unconscious but his wife still jerks him off to completion and he blows a load of blood. I don't want this to happen to me. I purge these thoughts from my mind and reason that I need to get this out of the way. Sooner or later I have to blow a load, and it's going to be now.

I picture Holly's asshole when she's sitting on my face, and I get back to work. When I'm about to cum, I power through the momentary apprehension and blow a load all over my hands and stomach. The orgasm itself doesn't feel any better or worse than normal. I let it settle and wait for any tinge of pain to set in my balls or dick or abdomen. There is none. I look at the load. It's white—completely normal. It's actually a little bigger than normal, but I assume this has to do with not cumming for a week.

I wipe my hands off on the sheets and use a pillowcase to clean the cum off my stomach. The best thing about living in a hotel is you can blow loads all over the sheets if you want and they'll be clean and changed by the time you're back from work. I could never count on that with Alyna.

chapter twenty-eight

Old Man on Campus

It's Saturday. I haven't talked to Alyna or my kids in a few days. I wonder when I'll see them next and I wonder what they think of me being gone. I try to put it out of my mind as I drive to CSUN. Holly is involved in a charity fundraiser to get credit for some class. She's running a booth selling cupcakes at a fair on campus, and she's asked me to show up and buy a few cupcakes. This will obviously lead to fucking, so I decide to oblige.

I ask the guy at the parking structure for directions, then park my car and start walking toward the fair. For some reason I expected there to be more of a family presence at the fair, but everyone involved—the people running the booths and the people buying things there—are all students. I'm the oldest person there by fifteen or so years. I assume they'll all think I'm a professor.

I meander around through the booths for a minute before zeroing in on Holly's. She's wearing a skin-tight skirt and a shirt that pushes her tits up and out. Even though I think about fucking almost every other female student I see walking around the place, it's clear that

Holly is the hottest of them all—and I personally know she can fuck like a maniac, so my fantasies involving her are much less fantasy than actual memory. I wonder if the other girls on campus fuck like her. I assume they probably do, given that they were all raised on porn.

I go up to Holly's booth and say, "I'll take a cupcake, please."

She smiles and says, "Hey, you made it."

I say, "I told you I'd be here."

She says, "Well, thanks for coming," hands me a cupcake, then says, "That'll be five dollars, please, sir."

I hand her the cash and take the cupcake, then say, "When are you relieved of your duties here?"

She looks at her phone and says, "In about an hour. If you want to hang around, check out some of the other things. We can hang out after."

Knowing there's a high probability of me getting my dick sucked if I hang around, I say, "Cool. Just text me when you get done."

I lean in to kiss her on the cheek. She pulls back a little but allows it. Her inability to return physical affection is strange to me. I try not to question it too much. I say, "See you later," then take my cupcake and walk around a little bit.

I look at all the booths raising money for various charities. I have no interest in any of them, so I walk a little farther away from the charity fair and take a seat near a fountain and start eating my cupcake. As I eat it I watch the students walk around me and try to remember what it was like to be that young, what it was like to be in college and not really know about bills or a mortgage or having kids or any of it. I can't. I remember specific things about my college experience— professors I had, chicks I fucked, a few parties I went to—but I can't remember what it felt like. I can't remember what my attitude about life was. I can't remember what I thought my life would be like when I became the age I currently am. I'm pretty sure I didn't think it would be what it has become, though. I wonder if any of the kids I see walking around think about what their lives will be like when they're my age and I wonder if any of them are accurate in their expectations.

I finish the cupcake and walk around campus. The girls all walk around staring intently at their phones, oblivious to anything around them, which makes it very easy to stare at their tits and asses and imagine fucking them in their dorm rooms, which I assume are all like Holly's.

Later I get a text from Holly asking me to meet up with her at her cupcake stand. I do, and then we head back to her dorm room and I fuck her in the ass, then she sucks my dick until I cum down her throat. I wonder if I'll remember how I felt on this exact day in another fifteen years, or if I'll just remember the event.

chapter twenty-nine

My Plus-One

Carlos and I are eating lunch. After divulging all of the recent events of my life to him, he says, "So you literally and figuratively got your balls cut off."

I say, "My balls were not cut off."

He says, "I was making a joke, you stupid fuck."

I say, "So, anyway, it's obviously just going to be me coming to your wedding solo."

He says, "Oh no, motherfucker. We already paid for the caterer and we put you down for two plates."

I say, "I'll pay you back."

He says, "It's not even about that."

I say, "Then why did you say it was?"

He says, "Don't be a dick. Look, you know I love Alyna, and I sincerely hope you two work everything out, and I have the utmost faith that you will. That said, just bring your new fucktoy."

I say, "I don't know about that, man."

He says, "Why not?"

I say, "It's still kind of new. It might be overstepping some bounds or something. I don't want her to think I'm trying to replace my wife with her, you know?"

He says, "You're so fucking stupid. If you went on Craigslist right now and fucking posted something that was like, 'Recently separated straight asshole seeks a lady to take to a wedding in Boston and please be ready to fuck and suck dick, also it's a gay wedding,' you'd be drowning in a fucking tidal wave of pussy."

I say, "What the hell are you talking about?"

He says, "Straight women love weddings, and the cool ones—which, from everything you've told me about this little minx, she seems like she's cool—fucking love gay weddings. When you invite her, don't say, 'Hey, come to this wedding with me and I'll make you my next wife.' Just say something like, 'Hey, I have to go to one of my best friend's weddings and I'd love for you to be my date. And, just to let you know, it's a gay wedding.' You just showed me her picture. She's hot. Hot chicks love gay guys. That little bitch's panties will be wet in a second."

I say, "I don't doubt that chicks like weddings, asshole. I'm just saying I don't want her to think that I'm making a big deal out of it, you know, making it like we're in a relationship or anything."

He says, "And is that because you don't want a relationship with her, or is that because you don't want to scare her away by getting too serious too quick?"

I say, "I don't know. I don't really know much about anything right now. I just know that I'm not sleeping in my own bed anymore and I'm not fucking my wife anymore—"

He says, "But you weren't fucking her when you *were* sleeping in your own bed."

I say, "You know what I mean. And I'm not seeing my kids anymore. Yeah, I like Holly. I like fucking her a lot. But . . ."

He says, "But nothing. I want to meet this little homewrecker now, so you're bringing her. She's your plus-one. It's settled."

I say, "I'll think about it."

He says, "Well, thinking with your dick got you this far. Just keep doing it and you'll be fine."

When I get back to the office I stare at a picture of Holly's ass on my phone for a while. Then I stare at it in real life while she dicks around on Facebook just outside my office. I get some work done and think about whether or not I should take her to the wedding. At the end of the day, when she's walking out, I bring her into my office.

I say, "Hey, I know this might seem weird, but it's not. I just need a date to something and I'd love for you to be that date."

She says, "What is it?"

I say, "A wedding."

She lights up immediately and says, "Ooh. I'll get to wear a dress."

I say, "Yeah, and you'll get to have a little vacation, too," and I wait for her to start getting a little uncomfortable with the idea but she doesn't. She actually claps a tiny clap and makes a squealing noise.

She says, "Oh my god, a destination wedding?"

I say, "It's not like that exactly. It's in Boston and it's my gay friend Carlos and his boyfriend."

She hugs me. It's the first time in a week that she's shown me any physical affection that was unsolicited and not overtly sexual. She says, "This is going to be so fun. I can't wait. I love gay guys."

In my hotel room that night, after we fuck, she curls up next to me and waits until I fall asleep to roll over to the other side of the bed, instead of doing it immediately after I blow my load, the way she usually does.

chapter thirty

Remnants

After lunch, I get an e-mail from Alyna informing me that I should drop by the house after work and pick up anything I might need or want because she's moving all of my shit into storage the following day. This is the first practical step she's taking toward a formal separation. It makes me feel shitty, but I'm not ready to stop fucking Holly. I feel like I need to hang on to that for as long as I can. But this certainly makes it seem like I'll have a much more limited amount of time to fuck her than I previously thought if I have any chance of salvaging my marriage.

When I get to the house—my house, the house I have made every mortgage payment on—I sit in the car and look at it for a few minutes. I remember the day we moved in and ordered pizza and fucked on the living room floor because we didn't have any furniture yet. I remember the day we brought Andy home from the hospital. I remember the day Jane took her first steps and smashed her head on the coffee table. It doesn't feel any different to me. It's still my house. I just don't actually live there anymore.

I walk up to the front door and take out my keys. I look at the lock and then put them back in my pocket and ring the doorbell. Now it feels different.

Alyna answers the door holding Jane in one arm. Andy's hiding behind her leg. When he sees it's me he yells, "Daddy! Come in!"

I try to lean in and kiss Jane, but Alyna spins around so I can't get to her. I give her a look that basically says, 'I know this is shitty, but do you really have to be that much of a cunt?' But I can't blame her, and I even kind of admire her for being so protective of our kids. It makes me feel like, even if she kicks me out for good, files for divorce, and never lets me back into the kids' lives, they'll be okay. She'll take care of them.

I bend down and pick up Andy. He kisses me on the cheek and says, "You work a real lot, Daddy." I say, "I know. Things have been really busy." Obviously Alyna still hasn't told them anything about what's actually going on. She can put my shit in storage and force me to live in a hotel, but until she tells the kids what's actually happening I think she's probably holding out some hope that we can resolve this.

Andy says, "Do you want to watch *Toy Story* with me?"

I look at Alyna. She shakes her head. I don't see any reason to piss her off further or to make this any more uncomfortable than it has to be. I say, "I'd love to, bud, but I have to get back to work. I just stopped by to pick up a few things."

Andy says, "Oh, then I'll wait until you get back from work to watch it. I want you to see it, too," and I start tearing up. I almost lose my shit right then and there. But I hold it together. I think about whatever I can that makes me mad. I think about what an asshole Lonnie is. I think about the bank losing one of my deposits. I think about Sherri Shepherd. These thoughts push the tears back as I put Andy down and head back into the bedroom. Alyna and the kids stay in the living room.

I see that the picture of the entire family we used to have up in the hallway has been taken down. In its place is a picture of Alyna and

Andy in the park. It's a picture I took but I'm not in it. I open one of my drawers in our dresser and absentmindedly toss some T-shirts into a duffel bag. I look at our bed and wonder if I'm ever going to sleep in it again. In the bathroom I grab some deodorant and razors to make it look like I'm actually taking things I'll use, even though I've already replaced these things.

I look next to the toilet and see that Alyna hasn't gotten rid of my magazines yet. I wonder if this is a sign of hope that everything will work out or if it's just something she hasn't gotten around to yet.

I turn the bedroom light off and head back out to the living room with my bag full of shit I don't need. Alyna says, "You got everything?"

I say, "Yeah."

She says, "I'll e-mail you to let you know which storage place I end up using."

I wonder if this is a bluff. It seems crazy to me that she's going to actually go through all the shit in the house, separate it into piles of mine and hers, and then hire movers to take all the shit she recognizes as mine to some storage place. I wonder about things like the couch or the chair that only I sit in. I don't ask her about these things.

Andy's watching us. I whisper quietly enough so he won't hear, "Do you think I could come by and just see the kids this weekend or something?"

She whispers back, "I don't know. I just don't know. Do you have everything you need?"

I say, "Yes."

She says, "Okay, then, you should be going."

I say, "Okay," and give my son a hug and a kiss before I leave. I lean in to give Jane a kiss and this time Alyna allows it. As I'm walking out the door Andy says, "Work fast, Daddy."

I say, "I will," then walk out the door.

I hear Alyna lock it behind me then I walk to the end of the driveway and toss the duffel bag into the trash can.

Blowjob Ass Cramp

I wake up to Holly stroking my cock. I reach down and start rubbing her clit until I can feel her pussy get wet, then I finger her a little bit. She starts fucking my finger, which is one of the hottest things she does. She actually grabs my hand and starts using it like a dildo, dictating the pace and strength with which I ram my fingers into her pussy.

She takes my fingers out and goes down on me, flipping her own body around so she settles her ass right in my face, and after being awake for less than a minute I'm staring at the most perfect ass and pussy I've ever dealt with. This makes it difficult to remember that my life is falling apart.

I lick her clit and she sucks my dick for a few minutes then she starts grinding her pussy on my face. I also find this incredibly hot. The momentum of her grinding causes us to slide slowly to the edge of the bed, and at some point I'm forced to hang one leg off and put my foot on the floor to support us so we don't fall onto the ground.

She stops sucking my dick and starts jerking me off, which I've come to know means that she's about to cum. I grab her ass as hard as

I can and pull her pussy down onto my face so I can eat her out properly while she cums, really get my whole mouth on it. I can tell by her moaning that she's close and that's when I feel it. A shooting pain tears through my left ass cheek. It's so painful that not only can I not ignore it, but it causes me to throw Holly and her perfect pussy off my face and ball up in the fetal position on the bed.

Holly says, "What's wrong? Did I do something wrong?"

Through gritted teeth I manage, "No. I have a cramp."

She says, "Where?"

I say, "My ass."

She says, "Like your . . . asshole? Or your ass cheek?"

I say, "My cheek," and try to laugh through the pain.

She says, "Which one?"

I say, "Left."

She starts rubbing it and laughing. I laugh a little, too, as I put my leg straight out in an attempt to stretch the muscle. Eventually the pain subsides and I take a deep breath. She says, "Better now?"

I say, "Yeah, I think so. Jesus fucking Christ that hurt."

She says, "Well, are you okay?"

I say, "Yeah, yeah. I'm good."

She says, "Good, because you're not finished," then she climbs back on top of my face and starts grinding her cunt on my mouth while she sucks my dick. I get hard almost instantaneously as I stare at her asshole. She cums easily, but it takes me a few minutes because I can't stop wondering if she'll be telling her roommate that the guy she's fucking is so old he got a cramp in his ass while she was sucking his dick.

chapter thirty-one

Gay Wedding

Carlos picks Holly and me up from the airport. The first words out of his mouth are to Holly. He says, "Holy shit, you are fucking gorgeous. What in the hell are you doing with this asshole? Kidding." He's more fired up than usual. I assume this is because he's getting married and because he's gay. I assume a straight man would not be this excited in the same situation.

He gives me a hug and whispers in my ear, "Fuck her every chance you get until it crashes and fucking burns. She's the hottest piece of ass you'll ever have in your life." Then he backs up and says to both of us, "Car's over here. Let's go."

I give Holly the front seat and get in the back. As I buckle my seatbelt, I say, "We're at the Marriott in town."

Carlos is about to start the car. He turns around and says, "What?"
I say, "The Marriott."
He says, "You stupid piece of shit. You're in the group that's staying at Teddy's aunt's house. I told you that."
I say, "No, you didn't."

He whips out his phone and scrolls through some text messages. He reads, "Hey, Teddy and I want you to stay at his aunt's house when you come out. You'll have your own room. Then you respond, 'Okay. Thanks. Sounds good.' Real fucking wordsmith."

I say, "Oh, sorry, man. A lot going on, as you know. I guess I forgot."

He says, "Well, un-fucking-forget. Cancel your room. We're going to the house." I cancel the room on my phone.

The conversation as we drive is mostly between Holly and Carlos. He asks her about herself. Some questions are things I've never thought to ask her myself. Her answers to these questions are exactly what I would have predicted.

When we get to the house Carlos shows us upstairs to our room. He says, "This is you guys. You have a bathroom connected to the room with a shower attached. You're the first ones here other than me and Tedward, but later when some more people get in we're all going out to a bar or something. Some shithole he went to when he was in high school. So get your party hats on." He turns to leave and then turns back. "Oh, and another thing. We're all adults here so I'll just be blunt. I know you two are going to fuck. When you do, put a towel down on that vent, because these vents are like a fucking PA system to every bedroom." He shuts the door behind him as he leaves.

I start unpacking and Holly goes into the bathroom and comes out with a towel. She tosses at it me. I catch it and say, "What're you doing?"

She says, "I've never fucked in Massachusetts before." She starts unbuckling my belt as I put the towel on the vent and try to make sure it's totally covered. She pulls my pants down and puts my entire dick in her mouth. It takes about three seconds for me to get a hard-on. She says, "I love when your dick gets hard in my mouth," then she hikes up the skirt she's wearing and I see that she's not wearing any underwear. I say, "Were you wearing underwear on the plane?"

She says, "No and you didn't do anything about it."

I say, "I didn't know I was supposed to."

She says, "You're always supposed to," then bends over the edge of the bed so I can see her pussy and her asshole. She licks a finger and reaches between her legs to lube up herself up with her own saliva. She reaches her hand up toward her mouth to lick it again and I say, "You don't need to do that," then get down on my knees and lick her pussy from behind while I grab her ass and pull it back into my face. It amazes me that no matter how many times I fuck her or grab her ass or see her ass from an inch away I'm still mesmerized by it. I wonder if, when she's Alyna's age, after she's had a kid or two, it will be covered in cellulite. I can't imagine that ever being the case.

Once her pussy is wet, I stand up and head over to my suitcase to get a rubber.

She says, "What are you doing?"

I say, "Getting a rubber." Even though I've had by balls clipped, I still haven't been in to have my sperm count evaluated and I'd fucking hang myself if I was the guy who got a chick pregnant after he had a vasectomy. I also haven't told Holly about it, and, even though it probably wouldn't matter at all to her, I'd rather just have her never know.

She says, "Just fuck me until I cum and then I'll suck you off."

We haven't had the "do you have any diseases?" conversation, and I'm pretty sure it would kill the mood if I initiated it at this moment, so I decide to roll the dice. At the very least, I'm pretty sure I can't get her pregnant.

I move behind her and slide my dick in. It's the first pussy I've had my dick in without a rubber in more than two years. I almost blow my load immediately. I'm reminded of high school. My girlfriend went on the pill shortly after we started fucking and the first time I fucked her doggy-style without a rubber I came in about three strokes. I've never done heroin, but I imagine that shooting it straight into your dick might feel something like fucking Holly without a rubber. I slow my pace and try to think about weird shit to make this last a little longer.

She moans a little too loudly and I say, "Shhh. Be quiet."

She says, "Make me."

As I fuck her, I reach up and push her face down into the bed. She moans again, but it's muffled by an old quilt. I wonder if Tedward's aunt made it, if it's a family heirloom or some shit. I wonder if anyone else has been fucked in this manner on it, maybe Tedward's aunt, maybe Tedward.

She presses back against my hand with her head so she can get her mouth unobstructed enough to say, "Put a finger in my asshole." Then she collapses back into the bed under the weight of my arm pushing her head down. I move the hand that's holding her hip toward her asshole, slide a finger along the side of her pussy, which is dripping, to lube it a little, and then push it into her perfect asshole. She cums and as she does, she writhes around with such force that I can't keep her head down. She screams, "Finger my asshole. I'm cumming! Oh, fuck! You fuck me so good."

Then she spins around and puts my dick in her mouth. She alternates sucking it and saying things like, "Cum down my throat," "I want to taste your cum," "Fuck my throat," and "I love how my pussy tastes on your cock." After a minute or so she reaches up and squeezes my balls as my entire dick is down her throat, and I cum harder than I think I ever have in my life. She swallows it all and then says, "That was fucking hot."

From the vent I hear Carlos's voice say, "Not too bad for straight people."

Holly's eyes get big and she covers her mouth in mock embarrassment. I laugh, take the towel off the vent, and say into it, "Sorry."

Through the vent Carlos says, "Put a towel down. I told you."

I say, "We did."

He says, "Well fuck quieter then."

That night we meet the six or seven other people who are staying in the house. Some are Tedward's cousins, Carlos's friends, and Tedward's aunt's friends. After a nice dinner cooked by Tedward's aunt, we all go to the bar Carlos mentioned. It's called Machine, and once we get there I realize it's a gay bar that's gayer than anyplace Carlos has ever tricked me into going to in LA.

I spend most of the night drinking beers and talking about movies with one of Tedward's straight cousins, a guy named Jim. Holly loves the place. She leaves her drink and her purse with me and Jim while she dances with Carlos and Tedward and other random gay guys in the bar. Every once in a while she'll come back to the booth to take a sip of her drink and say something like, "This is so much fun. I can't even believe it." I track her enjoyment of the night on my phone. She posts an update to Facebook every few minutes detailing the songs that come on the bar and how much fun she's having dancing with "her gays." Each post gets at least twenty responses, most of which are from guys.

As the night winds down, Holly is a drunken, sweaty heap leaning against me near the bar. She says, "When can we go? I want to fuck and sleep."

I look around for Tedward, who drove us here. He and Carlos are at the opposite end of the bar talking to some random guy, who I assume is gay based on his refusal to remove Tedward's hand from his ass. My suspicion is further confirmed when he makes out with Carlos in the car all the way back to Tedward's aunt's house.

Once we get back, Holly and I take a shower and I put down two towels on the vent, knowing that when she's drunk she's especially loud when we fuck. We get in bed and she starts jerking me off and saying, "Tonight was so much fun. Thank you for taking me to this. Fuck my ass."

Before I can respond I hear the same phrase repeated, but not by Holly. From under the stack of two towels I put over the vent I distinctly hear Carlos's voice say, "Fuck my ass." I assume Holly heard it too, since she stops the hand job she's giving me.

She says, "Did you hear that?"

Before I can respond to this, Tedward's voice comes out of the vent. He says, "Yeah, fuck his ass while you suck my dick."

My cock immediately goes flaccid and Holly takes her hand away. She says, "Oh my god. Are we listening to a gay three-way?"

I say, "Yeah. And two of the participants are getting married tomorrow."

She says, "I like gay guys and everything, but is it okay if . . . I mean, I don't think I can have sex while we're listening to this."

I say, "Totally fine. I'm right there with you."

I don't know if it's the amount she's had to drink, or if it's some deeper psychological freedom she's allowing herself to enjoy because she's on some kind of a vacation or at least not in the town she lives in, but instead of rolling to the other side of the bed to sleep without any physical contact from me like she usually does, Holly curls up next to me and falls asleep in my arms. It's nice. It's so nice I almost don't notice Carlos say, "I want to suck the cum out of your asshole," just before I drift off to sleep.

The following morning Holly and I wake up, shower, go downstairs and watch a little TV, and talk with some of the other people staying there until it's time to get dressed for the wedding. I usually don't notice clothes of any kind, but the dress she's wearing hugs her body like a fucking glove. She looks like a fucking model walking in front of me and she looks back over her shoulder and smiles. It's right then that I know I'll remember this exact moment for the rest of my life. Whatever may or may not happen with us in the future, I know I'll always have this image of her walking ahead of me with her perfect body outlined by that dress and her beautiful eyes and her smile. I wonder if I have these moments with other girls. I quickly go down the list of girls who were significant in my life and I can think of two other moments.

One was with Casey, my girlfriend before Alyna. We were sitting on the couch in my old apartment watching TV when a commercial came on for a bank or tax-preparation software or something similar, something to do with money. The commercial featured a bunch of chimpanzees in business suits tearing apart an office, and the tagline asked, "Do you know who's handling your money?" The question was rhetorical, but I answered it out loud by saying, "Monkeys?" Casey thought it was the funniest thing she'd ever heard. She laughed for a solid two or three minutes and I couldn't help laughing at her laughing. In a very concrete way, it was probably one of the happiest moments of my life.

The other was with Alyna. It has nothing to do with our wedding or with our kids being born or any of the crazy shit we went through in the beginning of our relationship. I used to drive anytime we went anywhere, and I used to open the passenger's-side door for her whenever we got into the car. One weekend, before we were married, we took a trip to Santa Barbara and she drove. When we went out to the car, she opened the passenger's side door for me. It was just a simple, stupid thing—I think she even did it as a joke—but I know I'll never forget it.

I sit down next to Holly and take in the decorations and the people in attendance. I assumed that a gay wedding, especially one involving Carlos, would be crazier—maybe sequins and disco music or something—but that's not the case. The decorations are all extremely normal; there are no guests in rhinestone jumpsuits or anything. It's tasteful, which is disappointing.

The wedding goes off without a hitch. No cell phones go off. Carlos and Tedward both remember their vows and cry at the appropriate times. No crazy guy lovers from the past interrupt the wedding. It's all very tame. Once they're pronounced husband and husband, they kiss and everyone stands up and claps. They walk back down the aisle into the house and Tedward's aunt says, "Please, everyone, stick around for dinner and drinks to be served right here in the backyard."

The catering service starts moving chairs and bringing out tables and the DJ sets up a little dance floor and his turntable. All of the guests meander toward the garden area, where there are a few bars set up. Holly and I proceed to get drunk and eat. At one point during the dinner she looks at me and says, "I know I already said this, but seriously, thank you. This is like the coolest thing I've ever been to with a guy," and for the first time since I've known Holly I see the possibility of something real with her.

I say, "Any time."

After dinner, the DJ starts playing music and the reception is not as disappointing in terms of blatant gayness as the ceremony itself was. Gay guys are having movie-style dance challenges with one another, and they're really good dancers. Gay guys are making out in the bushes. Carlos and Tedward are drunk and in love, slow-dancing to songs that shouldn't be slow-danced to. It's a spectacle.

At one point Carlos comes up to Holly and me and says, "Thank you so much for coming to this. Really. It means a lot to me." Then he starts crying.

I say, "Hey, man. You know I wouldn't miss this."

He hugs me, getting snot and tears all over my jacket, then says, "You two need a picture." He takes out his phone and snaps a picture of me with my arm around Holly. Holly says, "Can you e-mail that to me?"

She tells him her e-mail address and he e-mails the picture to her, then says, "You two are so fucking cute." Then he pinches Holly's cheek and slaps me on the ass before wandering back onto the dance floor to find his new husband.

That night, after the reception winds down, Holly and I fuck, but it's not like we normally do. She gets on top of me and says, "Let's do it slow." She looks in my eyes the whole time and we kiss. After she cums, I half-expect her to say she loves me, but she doesn't. I wonder if she wants to. I wonder if she wants me to say it to her. I don't. We fly back to LA the next morning.

chapter thirty-two

Secondary Contact

I'm sitting at my desk, watching a douchebag from Sales named Trent Packer flirt with Holly out at her desk. He has no reason to be on our floor at all. It wouldn't bother me so much, but she seems to be receptive to his bullshit. She laughs at whatever stupid shit he's saying to her. She feigns interest in the other stupid shit he's saying. I try to tell myself that I shouldn't let this get to me, that she's not my girlfriend, that I have no claim, that I'm technically still fucking married. It doesn't help.

My cell phone rings. It's Andy's preschool. His teacher, Mrs. Banks, says, "Hello, is this Andy's father?"

I say, "Yeah."

She says, "Sorry to bother you at work. Your wife is listed as Andy's primary contact, but we couldn't get in touch with her. You know it's incredibly important to list the contact that is most likely to be available during the day, otherwise we end up spending a lot of time trying to contact that contact and we could just be trying to contact the secondary contact, which is what you are."

My heart is trying to bust through my throat. All I can think is that Andy fell off the monkey bars and split his fucking head open, or lost his arm in some weird merry-go-round accident, and this bitch is going on about the importance of who gets listed as the fucking primary contact. I say, "Right. Is Andy okay?"

She says, "Oh, heavens. Yes. I didn't mean to scare you. He's just come down with a touch of something and he seems to have, well . . . vomited a little bit. He's in the nurse's office now, and I was just calling so you can arrange to have someone pick him up."

I say, "Thanks. I'll be there as soon as I can."

As I drive across town, I build up a nice head of steam wondering where the fuck Alyna is and why she wouldn't have answered her phone when she saw it was a call from Andy's preschool. I conjure images of her fucking some other guy, which doesn't piss me off as much as it should, and not because I'm fucking someone else, too, but because I find that I just don't really care. I imagine her out at a brunch that went too long with her cunt friends complaining about what an asshole I am, and all of them agreeing with her as they suck down mojitos and put more cellulite on their asses. Then I imagine her dead. No matter how irrational it may seem, I imagine her in a twisted heap of metal on the freeway somewhere and I momentarily feel good, like a weight has been lifted off me. If she were dead, I wouldn't have to deal with any of this shit. I'd get the kids and the house and I could fuck Holly and that would be that. I tell myself that I don't actually hope she's dead, but I kind of do. It would just make life so much easier.

When I get to Andy's preschool, the nurse tells me that he's been drinking 7-Up and he's been complaining of a stomachache. When he sees me he lights up and says, "Daddy! I thought Mommy was going to pick me up."

I say, "I think she's busy, bud. You'll have to settle for me."

He says, "I like this better," and as much as I don't want either of my kids to get caught up in whatever shit goes down between Alyna and me, I'm glad he seems to be on my side. I say, "Come on. I'll take you home," and we leave.

Once we get in the car Andy says, "I feel better. Can we get McDonald's?"

I say, "Didn't you just puke?"

He laughs and says, "Yeah, and I pooped."

I say, "In your pants?"

He says, "No, Daddy, in the potty."

I say, "Okay. That's cool."

He laughs and says, "No, it's not. It's gross."

I say, "What do you want from McDonald's?"

He says, "Ice cream."

I say, "Okay," and kiss him on the cheek. My nose gets close enough to his face to tell that his mouth still kind of smells like puke.

As we're pulling away from the drive-thru, I get a call from Alyna. It comes through the car speaker, so Andy can hear it, too. She sounds frantic. She says, "I got four missed calls from Andy's preschool. Do you know what's happening?"

I say, "Yeah. Do you have Jane?"

She says, "Yes. Of course she's with me."

I say, "Good," knowing that not filling her in on what's going on with Andy is eating her alive.

After a second of silence she says, "Well, fucking tell me what's going on!"

Andy laughs and says, "Mommy, you said a bad word."

She says, "Oh my god. Did you abduct him?"

I say, "What the hell are you talking about?"

She says, "Why is he with you?"

I say, "Because he got sick at school and they tried calling you but you didn't answer so they called me. His *secondary contact*." I want to get into it with her, but not with Andy listening. I feel like I have a pretty firm hold on being his favorite parent and I want to keep it that way.

She says, "Well, you have to take him home right now."

I say, "We're on our way. See you in ten minutes," then I hang up on her.

Andy says, "Why was Mommy so mad?"

I say, "I don't know, bud. Sometimes people just get mad."

Andy says, "You never get mad, Daddy."

I say, "I'll never get mad at you."

As he smears ice cream all over his face I wonder how old he should be before I start trying to convince him to never get married.

What Never Was

I'm in bed in my hotel room watching the old *Seinfeld* episode where they lose their car in a mall parking garage and Jerry has to take a piss. Jerry gets caught by the security guard and then it breaks for a commercial. The first shot in the commercial is of Casey, my old girlfriend before Alyna. She's in a kitchen with two kids who are complaining that they never have anything cool in their lunch. She saves the day by tossing some fruit-roll-up things in their lunch sacks and then she smiles at the camera.

I haven't talked to Casey in a long time—years. She always wanted to get married. I wonder if she ever did, or if the closest she'll come to being a wife and a mother is that commercial.

I try to imagine what my life would have been like if I'd stayed with her instead of dumping her and winding up with Alyna. I see us living in a house much like the one Alyna and I bought. I see us having two kids much like Andy and Jane, maybe with fatter asses. I see us never fucking and I see me cheating on her with Holly. I realize it probably wouldn't have mattered at all which girl I ended up with, but I know that's wrong. There were times—there was a long time, in fact—when Alyna was nothing like Casey, when she was the opposite of Casey. For most of our relationship, in fact, Alyna was the best person I knew. The hottest, the dirtiest in bed, the smartest, the most fun to be around. Eventually that all changed, but for a time she was incredible. Casey had moments of incredible in the beginning, but she never lived in it like Alyna once did.

I think about e-mailing Casey just to see if she's with a guy, if she's married, if she's happy. Instead I jerk off to a memory of Casey going down on me in one of her friend's bathrooms when we first started dating, and I blow a spermless load all over my hand.

chapter thirty-three

Tagged

I'm on my way to pick up Holly from her dorm. She just finished writing a paper and she wants to celebrate by getting drunk and fucking. I have no problem with this form of celebration. I'm on the 405, listening to Crystal Castles, because it reminds me of the first time I went to her dorm room, when the music cuts out and my phone rings over my car's speakers. I look at the caller ID in the console screen and see it's Alyna. As much as I don't want to talk to her, I assume it's serious if she's calling me. I press the answer button on my steering wheel and she says, "So you took that little fucking whore to Carlos's wedding?"

I don't know what I should say. She obviously found out, but if she found out through hearsay, I might still be able to salvage this with some deft bending of the truth or some unabashed outright lying. I say, "What?"

She says, "I was supposed to go to that wedding with you."

There's something in the way she says that last bit, some outrage that I don't think she's earned the right to have, that really pisses me off. Carlos was always my friend. Alyna was only invited because she's my wife. In my head it makes perfect sense that I should be able to take whoever I fucking want to take to his wedding. I say, "I know you were, but things have obviously changed."

She says, "No shit, asshole. I just didn't think you'd take that little slut to a wedding I was supposed to go to. I thought you'd just go by yourself. But I forgot—you have no class."

I'm curious why she thinks I took Holly, and I want to see if there's any way out of this. I say, "Are you just assuming I took her?"

She says, "No, you stupid piece of shit, I saw a picture of you two together on her Facebook page."

I say, "Are you fucking stalking her on Facebook?"

She says, "Uh, no, dickhead. I'm not as hopelessly desperate to know everything you're doing as you think I am. She fucking tagged you in it and I got an alert."

I want to drive my car through the guardrail and go careening off the side of the 405 freeway into the 7-Eleven I'm passing. I say, "Oh."

She says, "*Oh* is right, dickhead. I don't know why I thought there might be some way for us to work this out, or salvage anything, at least for the kids' sake, but this little bitch has you so wrapped around her finger it's disgusting. I can't even think about you in the same way. You're like a different person. I mean, I never thought you of all people could get so warped by something so clichéd. And the sad thing is, you don't even see it. She's using you. She got a free trip to Boston out of it. I bet you buy her dinners and pay for all kinds of things. And what does she have to do for that? Suck your dick? Shit, sign me up."

And I lose any ability to maintain my composure. I'm fuming. I want to kick my windshield out and scream until my throat bleeds. I say, "You *were* signed up for that shit. But you stopped doing the dick-sucking part."

I can hear Alyna on the other end of the phone gasping or trying to speak or something, but no words come through my car's speakers for a few seconds. Then the phone call ends and Crystal Castles comes back through the speakers.

I drive angry all the way to Holly's place. When I get there, I don't mention how stupid it was of her to tag me in that photo on her Facebook page. I assume she wouldn't agree with me or even understand why I wouldn't want to be tagged, because she puts photos of everything she does on her Facebook page and tags everyone in them and they all seem to be fine with this. Privacy is a concept that has no meaning to Holly.

That night, as I fuck her doggy-style, I grip the back of her neck harder than usual. I want it to hurt a little. I want it to seem like punishment, or at least like I'm exerting control over her, but it just makes her cum faster than usual. When I blow my load in her face, making sure to get some in her eyes, she genuinely thinks it's hot, as evidenced by the way she wipes my infertile load out of her eyes with her fingers and then licks them.

On the drive back to my hotel room I contemplate deleting my Facebook account but realize that the damage is already done—and that without my Facebook account, I'd have no way of knowing how many guys want to fuck Holly besides me.

The Herpe

I'm taking my usual morning piss in my hotel bathroom, and when I jiggle my dick to get the last droplet of piss off, I notice a red mark on my shaft. I know what an ingrown pubic hair looks like, and this is definitely not that. It's too high up on my shaft even to be a hair at all. I immediately think that Holly gave me herpes when I fucked her without a rubber at the wedding.

I get slightly nauseated at the idea of having to tell any future sexual partners that I have herpes. I imagine the conversation I'd have to have with Alyna if we were to patch things up. I can't decide if it would be a deal-breaker for her or if she'd be happy because it would give her a legitimate medical reason not to have to fuck me.

I make an appointment with my doctor for lunch and spend the rest of the morning looking up pictures of herpes outbreaks on the Internet. Every image I come across is far worse than the thing on my dick, but I assume the images online are the worst-case scenario. I look at dozens of dicks and pussies that are covered in red blisters so thick you can't see the normal skin tone anywhere around the genital region. Despite all of my efforts I can't find any images of what an initial outbreak looks like, what to expect when you detect the first blister.

By the time I get to my doctor's office, I'm convinced that the spot on my dick is just the first in what is about to be a wave of hundreds of open lesions on my cock. He says, "So what's the problem?"

I say, "I noticed something on my penis this morning."

I expect him to recoil or to be disgusted in some way, but that's not the case. Without any visible reaction to me basically telling him he's about to have to look directly at another man's penis—and that the penis in question will have something on it that could potentially be the result of an STD—he says, "Okay, let's see it."

I pull down my pants and stand in front of him. He puts on some rubber gloves, then wheels a little stool over and sits on it as he leans in and gets a good look at what's on my dick. I look down to see a guy basically fondling my genitals but I'm too horrified of hearing him say, "Well, you've got herpes," to really think about how gay this seems.

After maybe ten or fifteen seconds he wheels his chair back, peels off the rubber gloves, and tosses them in the trash can. I'm still standing there with my cock out, lifting up my shirt like a little kid. He says, "You can pull your pants up." I do.

He says, "The good news is, you don't have an STD."

I say, "Jesus Christ. Seriously? That's not herpes?"

He says, "No."

I say, "Well, what's the bad news?"

He says, "There is no bad news."

I say, "Then why'd you say, 'The good news is'?"

He says, "Because I thought it was good news."

I say, "That phrase kind of implies that there's also bad news."

He says, "Oh. Sorry. No bad news."

I say, "Well, then, what is it?"

He says, "It's just a regular, tiny abrasion. You might want to, uh, take it down a notch on the frequency or the, uh, enthusiasm level when you masturbate."

I say, "You really think I did this to myself? I would have noticed that, I think."

He says, "Well, maybe it wasn't you. Maybe the wife was a little too worked up. Maybe a tooth got involved in a certain process, if you get my meaning."

And I think back to the last blowjob Holly gave me. She took my cock so far down her throat that she gagged, and I remember one of her back teeth digging into my cock a little too hard. It didn't stop me from throat-fucking her, but I'll bet that's what it was. I say, "I think I actually know exactly when it happened. Sorry for wasting your time."

He says, "No problem. Better safe than sorry with things like this. It's always good to have peace of mind. You might just want to put some Neosporin on it or something. But you should be fine."

On my way back to work, I remember back to a time when Alyna and I first started dating. I think she would have been capable of giving me a blowjob wound like this. I wonder if Holly will ever get tired of sucking dick. If she does, I wonder if I'll still know her when that happens. I hope not.

chapter thirty-four

Public Knowledge

My boss, Lonnie, knocks on the door frame of my office and says, "Need to talk to you for a second."

I say, "Okay." As he walks in, he shuts the door behind himself. My neck starts getting hot as I jump to the conclusion that he's going to fire me for some reason. Spending too much time on Facebook or looking up too many herpes websites are the first offenses that come to mind. I make a mental note that if I do have to get another job after this conversation I will only use my phone to look at non-work-related items.

He sits down across from me and says, "How to say this . . . um . . . Notice you and the new intern have, you know, been kind of close lately."

I have no idea if he knows I'm fucking Holly. I also don't know the company policy for shit like this. It's very possible, likely even, that this place has always had a no-fraternization policy and I just never knew it. Technically she's not an employee, though. She's an intern. I decide that's going to be my defense if he actually knows that we're fucking. If he doesn't, I'm fully prepared to tap-dance my way around the truth. I say, "Yeah. She's great. She works really hard and I've helped her on a few projects here and there. She's really been one of our best interns."

He smiles and says, "Not really what I meant."

I say, "Oh. Okay."

He holds up his left hand, takes off his wedding ring, and sets it on my desk. He says, "Been married for twenty-four years. Never cheated on my wife."

I'm starting to feel like the guy who stays behind before a hurricane, boarding up his windows and hoping for the best as the storm approaches. I'm fully prepared for Lonnie to dish out some holier-than-thou moral-superiority speech or something, and I'm also fully prepared to tell him to go fuck himself when he finishes. I may not know the company policy about fucking co-workers, but I know you can't preach religious shit at work.

He says, "First five years, maybe even first six or seven, were fine, fun even. But the last fifteen or so? Basically prison. Don't care that you're cheating on your wife. Don't care that you're engaging in questionable activities with an intern. Don't care about that. Do care about what it's like."

I'm beyond confused. I say, "What do you mean?"

He sighs and says, "Just want to know what it's like to . . . you know . . . with a girl who looks like that."

I've never had a conversation with Lonnie outside of the office. We've never talked about anything that wasn't exclusively work-related, beyond maybe some idle kitchen chat about the Super Bowl or the company Oscar pool or something. And now here he is, sitting across from me, apparently asking me to tell him what Holly's like when she fucks. I'm not even sure I'm hearing him correctly. I say, "Are you asking me to tell you what it's like to have sex with our intern?"

He says, "Not in graphic detail or anything. Just curious about what it's like."

He says that last bit with such a palpable sadness that I wonder: If

I hadn't started fucking Holly, if I'd just toughed it out with Alyna for another fifteen years, would I have ended up just like him? No matter what happens with Holly and me, or Alyna and me, this makes me glad I fucked Holly, glad I got to see what life was like outside the cage, if only for a little while.

I know what he wants me to say, and coincidentally it's the truth. I say, "It's great. It makes me feel happy and alive and young again in a way that my wife just isn't capable of."

He nods and slides his wedding ring back on. He says, "Some other guys around the office know."

I say, "Should I be worried about HR or anything?"

He says, "Not sure if there's company policy against it and don't really have a reason to look into it. Don't know and don't really want to know. Just thought you should know it's not really a secret, in case you were trying to keep it that way for the wife or anything."

I say, "Oh. Thanks."

He stands up, and before he walks out he says, "Just wanted to say thanks and keep up the good work."

I look at my wedding ring and wonder when the time will feel right to actually take it off.

chapter thirty-five

Chance Encounter

Holly and I are on our way to eat dinner after work. She told me she's never been to Wolfgang's in Beverly Hills and fancy restaurants make her want to fuck. So we're headed to Wolfgang's.

Before we go over the hill I stop at a gas station on Ventura to fill up. I leave the pump running and walk around to the passenger's side, open the door, and say, "I'm getting a pack of gum. You want anything to drink?"

Holly doesn't look up from her phone and says, "Maybe. I'll come in with you." Then I wait for probably thirty seconds while she finishes texting or updating her Facebook before she gets out of the car and we walk into the gas station.

She gets a Starbucks Frappuccino. I get a fruit-punch Gatorade 2 and a Snickers bar. As we check out, Holly says, "Ooh, can we get some Lotto tickets?"

I say, "Scratch-off or regular Lotto tickets?"

She says, "Scratch-off. Why would you get regular Lotto tickets?"

I say, "Because the regular Lotto gives out more money, to the tune of twenty million dollars or something."

She says, "But nobody ever wins that."

I say, "Yeah. Somebody does, every week almost."

She says, "You know what I mean," and I buy her some scratch-off lottery tickets and we turn to head back to the car. Just as we're walking out the door, I stop dead in my fucking tracks. My legs turn to lead and I feel like my stomach is exploding. Walking in through the same door Holly and I are walking out of are Alyna, Andy, and Jane. All I can do is to wonder why I didn't just get gas on the other side of the fucking hill. She sees us. A conversation is unavoidable.

Andy starts it. He says, "Daddy!" Everyone in the place turns their head and starts to watch what I know is going to be one of the worst moments of my fucking life. I wonder if either of the two guys in the place is cheating on his wife and feeling any sympathy for me in what is clearly a nightmare scenario for any guy who has ever cheated on his wife.

I say, "Hey, bud."

He says, "Who is this?"

I don't know what to say, exactly. Holly surprisingly jumps in with "I'm your dad's friend from work."

Alyna has never been violent but I can see that she wants to fucking cave in Holly's skull with the heel of her shoe. I'm glad the kids are with her or she might actually attempt it.

Andy says, "Oh. Hi. What's your name?"

Holly says, "Holly. What's yours?"

Andy says, "Andy."

Alyna's had enough of this shit and I kind of don't blame her. It's one thing that Andy clearly favors me in this whole thing, but I can see why she wouldn't want Holly developing any kind of relationship with him, no matter how rudimentary. Alyna says, "Okay, well, I have things to do with these kids, and I'm sure you have things to do with your kid, so good-bye."

What a fucking cunt. Holly is visibly pissed off, but she doesn't say anything. She just glares at Alyna. If I was watching this on TV or in a movie it would be amazing. As it happens, I'm watching it in the gas station I'm trying to leave. It is far less amazing.

I say, "See you later, then."

I just want to get in the car and start dealing with whatever it is I'm going to have to say in order to salvage the night and still get to fuck Holly in the ass when I hear Andy say, "Daddy, when will I get to see you again?"

I say, "Uh, I don't know."

He says, "I want to see you tomorrow."

I say, "Well, I'll have to see how work goes."

He says, "No. I want to see you tomorrow!" Now everyone in the place is focused on our little drama that's unfolding. No one wants to be a part of it. I feel like I have no choice but to lie directly to my son. I say, "Okay. I'll see you tomorrow."

He says, "You promise?"

I say, "Yeah, bud, I promise."

He hugs my leg and says, "I love you."

I hug him back and say, "I love you, too."

He says, "See you tomorrow," and we leave.

We get in the car and drive over the hill to eat steak. The only thing Holly says about it is, "Sorry if I acted weird or anything. Just, that comment your wife made about me being a kid—you don't see me that way, do you?"

I say, "No. Not at all," even though I kind of do.

I tell her she didn't act weird, and I thank her for being cool about it. She still seems pissed, though, so I assure her that I don't view her as a child at all. I tell her she's mature and has her shit together and is young, certainly, but not a child.

That night, after I blow my load in her ass, I lie awake next to her as she snores on the opposite side of the bed from me. I stare at the ceiling imagining what my son is doing. He's probably asleep, but I imagine him awake in his own bed, happy that he'll get to see his dad tomorrow. For the first time in my life, I despise myself.

Shitdick

I wake up the next morning and realize that I never even took a piss after fucking Holly in the ass the night before. I just rolled over after I blew my load and obsessed about how I'm ruining my children's lives until I passed out. I have to piss so bad I wonder how I didn't piss the bed.

Holly is next to me, still snoring, as I get out of bed and head to the bathroom. I nudge her on my way toward the pisser and say, "Time to get up."

Once in the bathroom, I turn on the light and look down at my dick as I piss. There's a dime-size piece of dried shit on the head of my cock. I've fucked girls in the ass before. When we first started dating, Alyna actually used to enjoy being fucked in the ass. Every once in a while, I'd get a little brown streak on my dick or something but nothing like this. I must have been pushing against a real, fully formed turd when I was fucking Holly. That's the only thing that could have caused such a large piece of shit to stick to the head of my dick.

I scrape it off into the toilet with a fingernail and contemplate telling her about it. I decide there's no point in telling her. The best-case scenario is that she'd laugh it off, but worst-case she'd get embarrassed and never let me fuck her in the ass again.

As soon as I finish pissing, I turn the shower on. I'm about to get in when Holly knocks on the door and says, "Hey, would you mind if I used the bathroom before you got in the shower?"

I say, "No," turn off the shower, open the door, let her in, and go sit on the bed knowing that when she says, "I need to use the bathroom," instead of "I have to pee," it means she has to take a shit pretty bad.

chapter thirty-six

You Got Served

I'm sitting in my office, smelling my fingers and face, because even though I took a shower, I can still smell Holly's pussy all over me. It reminds me of how my high school girlfriend's pussy smelled. I wonder if it's because Holly is so young that it smells like this. I mentally scroll through every chick I've ever fucked and realize that only Holly, my high school girlfriend, and my college girlfriend had this specific type of smell. I decide it has to be their youth and commit to the idea that, if Alyna and I fall apart for good, I'll only fuck girls under twenty-two if I'm able.

I cup the hand that I fingered her with the night before over my mouth and nose and inhale deeply. I catch a faint whiff of Holly's asshole, and I'm reminded of the shit she took this morning, which smelled so bad I could barely breathe when I went back into the bathroom after her to shave. My desk phone beeps and our receptionist says, "Your wife is in the lobby."

I say, "Okay," take one more sniff, and head to the elevator wondering why the fuck Alyna would come to the office but knowing that it's better to deal with whatever it might be in the lobby than on my floor.

I get out of the elevator and I see Alyna standing there with her sunglasses on. They're a pair of big Dolce & Gabbana sunglasses that I bought her for her last birthday. I wonder if she just forgot that I got them for her, or if she likes them so much that she's able to dissociate my involvement with them enough to continue to wear them. She's also holding an envelope, which I immediately assume contains photographs of Holly and me fucking, taken by some private detective she's probably hired with our joint bank account.

I say, "Hey."

She says, "Don't fucking *hey* me."

I look over at our receptionist and say, "Gina, could you give us a second?"

Gina says, "I'm sorry. I can't really leave my desk. The phones and all."

I look back at Alyna and say, "Can we go outside?"

Alyna says, "Why? So your receptionist doesn't find out you're fucking the intern? I think she has a right to know what kind of a dickhead she works with."

Gina laughs, not too loud, but she laughs.

I say, "Okay. Fine. What do you want?"

Alyna says, "Just to give you these," and she hands me the envelope.

I say, "What is this?"

She says, "Don't play dumb."

I say, "Photos?"

She says, "Photos? What? No, you retard. It's fucking divorce papers."

I say, "What?"

She says, "You didn't think I was just going to sit by, running into you and your little fucktoy at gas stations, and wait for you to figure out whatever kind of fucking midlife crisis you're going through, did you?"

I say, "I don't know. I mean, did you go to a lawyer?"

She says, "Well, yeah. I couldn't really draft up legal divorce documents on my own, now, could I?"

I say, "Well, I haven't been to one."

She says, "Then I suggest you go to one, because I want those signed soon. I'm tired of this shit." Then she walks out.

I look over at Gina, who's clearly pretending to be on a phone call that isn't really happening. I get into the elevator, go back to my desk, and start Googling divorce attorneys.

chapter thirty-seven

Another Chance Encounter

Holly and I are walking around the Westfield Promenade. I'm trying to eat my own ice cream while holding hers because she needs both hands to reply to some Facebook messages about an upcoming birthday party for one of the girls she goes to school with. It's difficult.

While looking at her phone, Holly says, "I just, I don't know. I like this girl, but I don't know if I want to spend next Saturday night at her place, you know?"

I say, "Uh-huh."

She says, "Oh, look, though. James is going. Tina is going. Sarah is going. Maybe it won't be that bad. Should I go?"

I say, "If you want to."

She says, "Would you want to go?"

I say, "If I were you?"

She says, "No. If you were you."

I say, "You mean, like, go with you to this party?"

She says, "Yeah. Would that be weird for you?"

I say, "No. Why?"

She says, "Because you're, like, old, you know?"

I say, "I don't care if you don't," and find that I honestly mean this. I'm flattered that she'd ask me to be her date to a party with friends her age. Some part of me has always thought she wouldn't tell any of her peers about me because she'd be embarrassed. This is concrete proof that she wouldn't be. I say, "Actually, I'd love to go."

She says, "Okay. I'll tell her we'll go then."

I finish my ice cream as we approach a trash can and say, "You want any more of yours?"

She says, "Nah," and I toss both of them toward the can. Hers goes in, but mine, the empty one, banks off the lip of the can and hits the floor. Holly bends over to pick it up and I take the opportunity to give her a playful slap on the ass. As she stands back up, some guy throwing his drink away at the same trash can sees me slap her on the ass.

He says, "Holly?"

She looks up and says, "Dad?"

I have an immediate urge to walk away from the situation or fake passing out so I don't have to deal with what is about to occur. Instead I look at Holly's dad and the woman he's with, who I assume is her mom. They're older than me, but not by much. I certainly look closer to them in age than I do to Holly. I wonder if she's told them about me.

Her dad puts out his hand and says, "Hi, I'm Roger. And you are . . . ?"

I introduce myself and shake his hand with the hand that was just on his daughter's ass. I wonder if he notices this.

Her mom remains silent as her dad and I have a brief conversation about nothing. After maybe thirty seconds, Holly says, "Well, we should be going."

Holly's dad says, "Okay, nice to meet you. Holly, you still coming to the house tomorrow?"

She says, "Yeah."

He says, "Okay, see you then," then leans in and kisses her on the cheek in what I can only assume is some kind of weird power play to mark his territory. There's no way he knows that I've had my dick in every one of his daughter's holes, but he has to suspect.

As Holly and I head to the parking structure to get in my car I wonder if I'll ever have to deal with something like this with Jane when she gets older. I wonder if I'd care if she was fucking a guy fifteen years older than her. I wonder if that guy would have a wife he was cheating on, too, and two kids whose lives he was ruining.

John Larroquette

I just came on Holly's tits and she's in the bathroom cleaning up. I turn on the TV and flip through the channels until I land on an old episode of *Night Court*, guest-starring a young Teri Hatcher. She plays a woman who's trying to get Dan Fielding to fuck her, but he won't because she's the niece of one of his clients.

Holly comes back in from the bathroom and gets in bed with me. She says, "Is that the old lady from that one show?"

I say, "*Desperate Housewives*. Yeah. Her name's Teri Hatcher."

We watch for a few minutes. She says, "That guy is funny. What is this show?"

I say, "*Night Court.*"

She says, "How old is it?"

I say, "It's from the eighties."

She says, "Like when *Fresh Prince* was on? Or was that the nineties?"

I say, "Nineties."

She says, "What's that guy's name?"

I say, "John Larroquette."

She says, "He's seriously funny. Did he die or something?"

I say, "No. Why?"

She says, "Because he never did anything else."

I say, "He's done a bunch of stuff."

She says, "Like what?"

I say, "He did a show called *The John Larroquette Show* that I think he won some Emmys for, and he's on a bunch of TV shows now. He did some *CSI* stuff. He's been on *Parks and Rec*."

She says, "Seriously? Are you making that up?"

I say, "Why would I?"

She says, "To be funny."

I say, "How would that be funny?"

She says, "It wouldn't."

We fuck again before we go to sleep, and as I pull out and blow my load in Holly's ass crack, I wonder if John Larroquette ever gets pissed off when he has to explain who he is to girls Holly's age.

chapter thirty-eight

Happy Fucking Birthday to You

After getting some green tea from the kitchen, I sit down at my desk and log on to Facebook to check the inane shit Holly has posted since I last looked. It's strange to have a pretty decent memory of each time she was doing something on her cell phone the last time we hung out and then be able to see each and every thing she was posting. It's the only thing that stops me from asking her what she's doing on her phone every time she's typing away in my presence.

As soon as I go to her page, I realize that it's unmistakably her birthday. There are forty-six posts on her wall, each with their own collection of comments all wishing her a happy birthday and asking what kind of presents she wants or where she wants to go out to dinner or how drunk she plans on getting. I had no idea it was her birthday at all. I scroll through all of the recent posts that have anything to do with her birthday, and I sleuth out a few things. Donald Himmel definitely wants to fuck her. Ken Grint definitely wants to fuck her. Tommy Hooper probably has fucked her, based on his comment, "Wish it could be your birthday eve two years ago. Bomb! Night. Up for a replay?" But beyond all this, I learn the most from one of her own comments to a post from Tony Berg that reads, "What chu need fur yer bday lady?" Holly replies, "My laptop is fried. Got a new one laying around hahaha?"

I don't know if Holly expects me to know that it's her birthday or not. We've never discussed anything remotely approaching the topic, but I can only assume that, because she knows I'm on Facebook and we're friends, she thinks I should know.

At lunch, I go to CVS and get her a card. I don't want it to say anything about love, but even though she swallowed a load of my semen less than forty-eight hours before this, I want the card to have a clear message of romance, so it doesn't seem like I'm just a friend. I find one with a flower on it that reads, "I'm so glad you are in my life. Happy Birthday!" This is perfect. I get some wrapping paper, some tape, and some scissors and head back to the car.

After CVS I drive through McDonald's and get lunch, then head to an Apple Store, where I have to deal with a teenager trying to upsell me on the most expensive laptop they have. I finally convince him that I'm unwilling to buy anything more costly than the bottom-of-the-barrel Macbook Pro, which is still fucking twelve hundred dollars. I reason that this will make Holly extremely happy, and the amount of fucking we've done has already been worth at least twelve hundred dollars, compared to the money I've spent on Alyna over the years versus the amount and quality of sex we've had.

Back in the car, I finish my fries, then do the worst wrapping job I've ever done in my life on Holly's new computer. When I get back to the office, I think briefly about waiting for Holly to go to the bathroom and surprising her by sitting the computer and the card on her chair. Thankfully I think this through to its logical conclusion, which involves far too many witnesses, so instead I send her an IM that reads, "Can you come into my office please?"

She comes in and sits down across from me. I say, "First of all, happy birthday," and I hand her the card. She smiles and says, "Ooh, thank you. I thought maybe you forgot."

This implies that I would have known before I forgot and confirms my initial suspicion that she expected me to know, even though we'd never discussed it. I don't bring this up. I wait for her to read the card in which I've written the following note:

"Holly, I know the circumstances aren't the best but I can't tell you how glad I am that I stayed late that night to help you in the file room. You've made me happier than I thought I could be since we met, and I just want you to know that you're very special to me and I'm excited to see where this goes. Happy Birthday."

I expect her to say something similar to me after she finishes reading it. I hope she'll tell me how important I am to her or how much she enjoys spending time with me. This is not the case. After she reads it she says, "Thanks. That's really cool," then she sits the card on the edge of my desk and stands up to leave.

I say, "I also got you a present."

This gets a big smile from her—a real smile. She says, "What? Really?"

I say, "Yeah," and pull out the computer.

She looks at it and says, "Should I unwrap it in here?"

I say, "Sure."

She unwraps the computer and almost shits her pants. She says, "Oh my fucking god. Are you even serious right now? A fucking Macbook?"

I say, "Pro."

She says, "Yeah, I don't think they make the regular ones anymore. This is so cool. I so need a new computer, too. Oh my fucking god. Thank you so much."

She hugs me and says, "Is it cool if I leave it in here, in your office until after work? I don't want to be messing with it at my desk."

I say, "Yeah."

She kisses me on the cheek and says, "Oh my god! Thank you so much," then heads back out to her desk.

I sit back down at my desk and look at the card I gave her, which she's left on the edge of my desk. I didn't spend much time crafting the message inside, but I'd still hoped it would produce some emotional reaction in her. I had hoped it would serve as a verbal admission of the affection that I've genuinely started to feel for Holly, and prompt a similar reaction from her. Instead it sits at the edge of my desk, just shy enough of the edge that it won't fall off. It reminds me of Holly sleeping on the opposite edge of the bed from me at night. I decide I'm reading too much into it, take out my phone, and cue up some pictures of her bending over and spreading her ass so I can see her perfect asshole.

chapter thirty-nine

The Biggest Fucking Shark

"This isn't going to be fun. Get that in your fucking head right now. You think things are bad now? Well, let me tell you, they get about a million times fucking worse. You have to know that moving forward. So, you're probably asking yourself, What is it that I can do for you? Fair question. Here's the answer. I can make it so when the dust settles, when the smoke clears, you're sitting as pretty as you can be after something like this. I can make it so your life is less miserable than it would be otherwise. And, most of all, I can give you the best possible foot to stand on once it's all said and done. And most other guys who do what I do won't tell you this shit. They'll tell you they'll get through this with you. They'll be your friend in all of this. They'll share the knowledge they have from doing this shit hundreds of times with you. Fuck that. I'm not your friend. I'm not your shoulder to cry on. And frankly, if I can be frank, I don't care what kind of emotional toll this takes on you. Because you're not paying me to be your pal. In fact, you're not paying me to *be* anything. You're paying me because I already happen to be what you need: a fucking shark. I'm the biggest fucking shark in the deepest part of this cesspool of an ocean we're all swimming in. Sure, there are other sharks. But they're small. They're weak. Maybe they'll take one of her arms or a leg or a chunk out of her ass. Not me. I'll eat that bitch whole and spit out the bones. Then I'll eat the fucking bones. And I know you're probably sitting here saying to yourself, 'This guy just referred to my lovely wife as a bitch.' That's right. She can be whatever you need her to be to you, but to me, she's a bitch, and I need to tear her apart. Because, like I said, when the dust settles and it's a year from now, do you want to be living in a studio apartment in the Noho Arts District? Or do you want to be living in a house in a nice suburb, maybe even the house she's currently kicked you out of? This is California, my friend. She gets half of everything right out of the gate because you failed to secure a prenup. Most other guys just try to minimize the damage and convince their clients to get it done as quickly and quietly as possible. That's a fucking mistake. I will fight and scratch for every fucking dime I can get, and I won't play nice. I'll hit this bitch where it hurts. You have dogs? I'll take a full week bargaining the custody of the dogs, until she's so tied up thinking about whether she's ever going to see Fido again that she just signs the cars over to you without a second thought. You got kids? I'll twist her little pea brain so tightly around the idea that maybe you'll get custody and she'll wind up with nothing but weekend visitation that she won't even understand what the hell's happening when she signs the house over to you. Play the emotional property against the financial property—shit works like a fucking charm every time. Most guys don't have the balls to do it. They don't have the balls because they're pussies and pussies don't have balls, my friend."

I say, "Well, thanks. It sounds like you're very capable and everything."

He says, "Understatement, but yes, I am."

I say, "Anyway, like I said, I'm still talking to a few more people—"

He says, "You have to. Even I recommend seeing what's out there. Get that peace of mind."

I say, "Right. So I'll let you know within the next day or two."

He stands up and shakes my hand and says, "In the end, it's obviously your choice who you want to go with on this thing. But make no mistake, I am the biggest fucking shark you'll meet in these waters. And when you have the biggest shark on your side, the other fish can't fuck with you."

I say, "That's very reassuring. Thanks again."

He says, "My pleasure," and I leave his office wondering if he has that entire speech memorized or if it's slightly different every time he delivers it.

chapter forty

Kid's Birthday Party

The entire time Holly and I eat dinner at Villa Piacere, she sits there checking Facebook to see who's going to be at her friend's birthday party. She looks up maybe twice, but she never stops talking. She says, "I thought this party was going to suck, but Joel Revoredo is going and it looks like he's bringing Anthony Iannucelli. They're fun. And Tim Lavalley is going. Oh wait, though, I think he quit drinking. Lame. Whatever. Ooh, Josh Thorpe. This actually looks like it might be pretty fun." I notice that all the names Holly mentions are guys.

As I get the bill, I say, "Seems that way."

She says, "Don't be a dick."

I say, "I'm not. I can't wait to meet all your friends."

She says, "You'll like them, I bet."

There is no way on this planet that I could possibly like them unless their parents just gave them guy's names but they're all actually chicks who look like Holly and have the same desire to fuck me in the same filthy manner. I've been curious about what her parents said about me since we ran into them in the mall. I say, "Hey, what did your parents say about meeting me?"

She says, "We didn't talk about it."

I assume this is a lie, but maybe not. Maybe they have the kind of relationship where the parents don't ask too many questions and she doesn't volunteer too much information. I say, "Okay. Just curious."

She says, "Oh, and Phil Dimp is going. This should be pretty fun. You ready to go?"

I say, "Just need to get my credit card back."

On the way to the party I listen as she keeps thinking of people who are going and reading me comments they're all making about the party. The most interesting of these is offered by a guy named Dan Carmine. Dan's comment reads, "Somebody better suck my fucking dick this time. I got snubbed at your birthday party last year. Hahaha."

Although Holly assures me this is a joke, I imagine a party full of twenty-year-old girls sucking random guys' dicks in every room. I had no such parties when I was twenty.

We pull up to the house, which is unmistakable because it's the only house on the street with a dozen or so drunken, screaming kids in the front yard. I fully expect to run into another set of parents who are closer in age to me than to the kids at the party. I say, "Are this girl's parents home?"

Holly says, "No. They're out of town."

I say, "Oh," and we get out of the car and head in.

Once inside, it's clear I'm the oldest person at the party by a solid twelve to fifteen years. I get a few stares from guys and girls. The girls are trying to figure out why I'm there and the guys are sizing me up. I put a hand on Holly's lower back to establish that I'm with her, and this seems to allay some of the concerns these kids appear to have about my presence.

Holly runs into some kid she knows and says, "Where's Katrina?"

The kid says, "Out back, I think. Smoking."

Holly says, "Cool," and we make our way through the kitchen to the backyard where another dozen or so kids are huddled around a keg smoking weed out of a pipe. Holly spots Katrina and makes a beeline for her, saying, "Katrina! Happy b-day! You did it!" I follow her to the group and wait to be introduced, but that never comes, because Holly and Katrina are too busy hugging one another and saying how much they've missed one another since the last time they hung out a month ago. I introduce myself to Katrina and say, "Thanks for having me out to your party. Happy birthday. Great house, by the way."

She says, "I guess. It's the one I grew up in. Thanks for coming, though. You smoke?"

I wonder what the mortgage is as Katrina offers me the pipe. I say, "Sure," take the pipe and look forward to feeling a little less uneasy in this strange party, which I know I'm far too old to be attending. I inhale as deeply as possible and launch into a coughing fit. A guy standing to my right pats me on the back and says, "You all right, man?"

I manage to cough out, "Yeah, I'll be fine."

Another guy taps me a beer from the keg and says, "Here, dude."

I take a sip and start to feel the weed kicking in. The party immediately begins to feel more fun. I look at Holly. She's whispering something to Katrina. I lean in to her ear and say exactly what I'm thinking: "You're fucking beautiful." I kiss her on the cheek. She laughs and says, "I'm going to go inside for a second. You cool out here?"

I feel like I am. I feel like these people, these kids, are my friends. I say, "Yeah, I'll be out here."

She heads inside and I introduce myself to everyone standing around the keg. They're all fellow CSUN students or friends of friends of CSUN students. Some of them know Holly, some don't. They ask me how I met Holly and I tell them. One of the guys who introduced himself to me as Zip says, "Fucking pimp, bro. I hope when I'm an old dude I can pull a piece of ass that hot." I take this as a compliment.

Zip and I discuss various things with input from some of the others, such as the nature of reality, the possibility of a microchip being implanted in your brain that will give you the ability to achieve instantaneous orgasm, and what is the strangest kind of pornography that each of us has seen. I perceive this conversation to have taken place over the course of at least an hour. I look at my phone and see that only fifteen minutes have passed since Holly and I got out of my car when we pulled up to the party.

A girl standing around the keg named Jill or Joan says, "So, you and Holly are cool together." This is not a question. It's some kind of strange approval, or at least that's how I'm hearing it.

I say, "Thanks."

She says, "Thanks," in the exact same inflection I did. I can't tell if my confusion is from me being high or from her being high. It doesn't matter. Jill or Joan says, "So, this might be like too depressing or offensive or something, but I'm going to ask it anyway."

I say, "Okay."

She says, "What's the worst thing about being old?"

I'm not offended in the least by this question. Maybe because I'm high, I approach the answer with the most earnest evaluation I can muster. I say, "You really want to know?"

Everyone around the keg has turned their attention toward me, toward the next words that I will speak, toward the prophecy about to be delivered by the wise old sage who's wandered into their celebration of youth. I say, "Realizing your potential is gone—that's pretty bad. But the worst thing is being okay with that. At some point you're going to wake up and you'll have a job that you don't like, but it won't be like other jobs you've had that you don't like. You can't quit this one and move on to another one, because now you're married and you have kids and you have bills. And you'll tell yourself that it's just temporary, that even though you're married with kids you still have time to get around to doing whatever it is that you wanted to do when you were young. But then the job stops sucking as much, and not because it gets better, but because you just stop caring. You get used to the routine. You give in. You realize that your life will never get better and you tell yourself that what you ended up with isn't so bad. It's not good, but it's not bad. This is it. This is what it's going to be until you can retire. And maybe you'll get to go on a cruise or something once the kids leave the house, but whatever you thought you'd be doing when you were young . . . you realize one day that you'll never do that thing, and then you eventually become okay with that. That's the worst thing about being old."

I take a drink of my beer as Zip says, "Fuck, bro. That's some hardcore shit."

I say, "Yes, Zip, that is indeed some hardcore shit," and pat him on the back.

We all smoke a little more and talk a little more about things that aren't as important or depressing. Eventually, I notice that Holly still isn't back. I say, "Katrina, where's the bathroom?"

She says, "There are some inside, or you can just piss out here on a tree or something if you want. And if you have to, like, shit, just don't do it in the upstairs bathroom that's attached to my parents' bedroom. My dad got super-pissed last time because somebody streaked his toilet."

I say, "Okay. Thanks," and head inside, partially because I do have to piss and partially because I want to find Holly and kiss her and rub her shoulders. As I think this, I tell myself to remember that I should definitely get a prescription for marijuana.

Once inside, I ask around if anyone has seen Holly. Someone says they saw her out on the front lawn with some other people, so I stop in the nearest bathroom, take a piss while looking down at Katy Perry on the cover of an *Entertainment Weekly* lying next to the toilet, then head out front. Holly is standing with a few other people. They're all laughing and having a good time, and whatever hesitation I had about coming to this party with her is gone. No one seems to care that I'm older than everyone, and I'm with the hottest chick at the party, so fuck them if they do.

I move up next to Holly and say, "Hey."

She says, "Hey."

I put my arm around her and lean down to kiss her. She's slightly hesitant but still kisses me. The kiss is bad. It's just a little peck on the lips. I wonder if it's because she doesn't want to be associated with me in front of her friends. I wonder if that's why she left me by the keg and disappeared for so long. Fuck that. I look at her and lean back in, forcing an open-mouth kiss with tongue. She obliges, but she doesn't seem comfortable, and I notice a strange taste in her mouth. It's something I find vaguely familiar. The taste is like a smell I know but can't quite place. I pull back from her and taste the inside of my mouth. She watches me intently. She says, "You okay?"

I say, "Yeah. You taste kind of weird. What is that?"

She says, "What's what?"

Then it hits me. My mind rushes back to a night when I was with my old girlfriend Casey and she was on the pill. After I blew a load in her pussy, she asked me to go down on her. I just licked her clit and tried my best to stay away from the hole I'd dumped my semen in, but some got in my mouth. And it definitely tasted exactly like the inside of Holly's mouth.

I look at Holly, and I can feel my head getting hot. My scalp feels like it's fucking melting. She can tell I've figured it out. I feel sick to my stomach. Not only did she suck some guy's dick at a party I gave her a ride to, but she let me lick his cum out of her mouth. I want to kill everyone at this party, starting with Holly. I don't know what to do. I don't know if I should make a scene right here, just start yelling at her right in front of everyone, or if I should play it cool. But I don't want to be the crazy old dude who went insane at a college party, and as hard as it is to tamp down my boiling, venomous rage, I say, "Nothing," and put my arm back around her like everything's cool.

We stay at the party for another few hours. I spend my time staring at every guy there like I'm going to rip his balls off and shove them up his asshole, in the hope that one of them will reveal himself. By the time we get back in my car, however, I've gained no conclusive information regarding the identity of the recipient of Holly's clandestine blowjob.

I wait for her to put her seatbelt on, then I say, "So. You sucked some guy's cock at this party."

She doesn't even try to deny it. With no apparent guilt, she says, "I'm sorry," as though I've offended her by even bringing it up.

I say, "You're sorry? I brought you to this party. I'm your fucking ride. And you sucked some other guy's dick."

She says, "Yeah. So what? I'm going home with you. Doesn't that count for anything?"

I say, "What? I mean, we never talked about being exclusive, but I guess I just assumed that, even if you were fucking other guys, you'd have the courtesy to do it more discreetly than fifteen feet away from me at a party I'm also attending."

She says, "First of all, I didn't fuck him. And I don't even like the guy, so chill out."

I say, "Then why'd you suck his dick?"

She says, "I owed him."

I say, "Wait. What?"

She says, "Do we really have to get into this?"

I say, "How can we not get into it? I tasted another guy's fucking cum in your mouth. I'd say we're about as into it as we can fucking get. I mean, I bought you a fucking MacBook."

She says, "I tried to stop you from kissing me."

I say, "That was very considerate. Now, please tell me what the hell you're talking about, *owing* this guy."

She says, "He used to deal me weed and I'd give him blowjobs. He floated me the last time, and I said I'd get him back the next time I saw him. I didn't know he was going to be at the party and he decided to collect."

I look at her. She's so hot that, for a split second, I can almost rationalize this. For a measurement of time that's almost imperceptible, I tell myself that if I don't get over this I'll never fuck her again. I can almost agree with her logic. I can almost see some value in the fact that she honored her bargain with this guy. Then reality takes hold again. I say, "I'm assuming this wasn't a one-time thing, then. You'll have to suck his dick again?"

She says, "No. I just get weed from my roommate now."

I say, "Do you get other things from other guys for blowjobs?"

And that's the line that puts it over the edge. She says, "Hey, I never said I was your girlfriend or anything. I can fuck anyone I want or suck any dick I want. We're not a couple."

I know this before she says it, but the impact of actually hearing her say it is difficult to withstand. She continues: "I don't know what you think is going on between us, but it's just fucking. I mean, I like hanging out with you and everything, and I like sex. I just don't let my emotions get involved in the sex part of things. So the guys I fuck, I fuck them because it's fun, and the guys I hang out with, I hang out with because they're fun. There's only a few guys that I do both with, and you're one of them. So if that's not enough for you, then I don't know what to tell you."

When I drop her off at her dorm we do not kiss.

Advice from a Pro

Todd calls me. He says, "You in the mood for a little booze?"

I am. I say, "Yes."

He says, "Forty-five minutes? Zons?" I meet him forty-five minutes later at the Four Seasons in Beverly Hills. It's a Sunday night, so it's not that crowded. A few out-of-town businessmen who didn't fly back to wherever they're from on Sunday morning sit around the lounge as Todd and I take two seats at the bar. We get our drinks and he says, "So, how you managing the shitstorm?"

I say, "Not too well, man. Alyna wants me to sign divorce papers and Holly sucked some guy's dick last night at a party that I drove her to."

He says, "By 'some guy' you don't mean you, right?"

I say, "I do not mean me."

He says, "Sorry, man. That's some real shit. I know I always say this, but seriously, thank you for constantly reminding me why I will never get married."

I say, "Fuck you."

He says, "Lighten up. This shit will all be behind you in a year or two."

I say, "I don't know if you remember that I have kids. So, no, it won't."

He says, "I know, man. I know."

I notice a woman next to us, dressed a little too slutty for the Four Seasons, sipping a Diet Coke by herself. She's wearing enough perfume so that I can smell her from where I'm sitting. She smells good. She looks over at an old bald guy sitting at the end of the bar, then slides down a few chairs so she's sitting next to him and she says, "Hey, how's your night going?"

I look at Todd and say, "You see that shit?"

He says, "Yeah."

I say, "You ever had a chick do that to you?"

He says, "Dude, she's a fucking pro."

I say, "What? How do you know?"

He says, "The Zons, the Peninsula, Beverly Wilshire—high-class pros hang out in the bars and pick up rich dudes who are staying in the hotel."

I say, "Are you fucking serious?"

He says, "Yeah."

I turn and watch the prostitute work her game on the old guy. She says, "You staying here?"

He says, "Yeah."

She says, "Very nice. I love this hotel."

He says, "Yeah. I stay here when I'm in town."

She says, "You leaving tomorrow?"

He says, "Yeah."

She says, "Well, you should make sure you have as much fun as you can on your last night here."

He raises his drink and says, "I think I'm just going to finish my drink and then go to bed." He fucking knows the drill. I wonder if he's fucked prostitutes before. Maybe he's even fucked this one before.

She says, "Okay. Well, it was nice to meet you." I wonder if she's fucked him before and doesn't even remember.

The old bald guy downs his drink, pays his tab, and heads off into the hotel. The pro looks around at her prospects, which are not too good, checks her phone, and then slides back over to us. In a tone completely devoid of any of the sexual charm she used on the old bald guy, she says, "How's your night going?" to Todd and me.

Todd says, "Not bad. You?"

She says, "Pretty slow." She's not completely divulging the fact that she's a prostitute, but she might as well be.

Todd says, "Can I ask you something?"

She says, "Sure."

Then, without even asking if it's okay with me, he says, "My friend here is going through a shitty divorce. Seems to me like you might know more than the average person about how relationships and shit like that work. You got any advice for him?"

Without skipping a beat she says, "Well, who cheated on whom?"

I say, "Uh . . . I guess technically I did the cheating."

She says, "But it was because the Mrs. wasn't sucking your dick anymore, right?"

I say, "In so many words."

She says, "And was the pussy you got worth ruining whatever you had with the Mrs.?"

I say, "I thought it might be, but I don't think so now."

She says, "So lesson learned. You fucked up. Do you think you fucked up?"

I really think about this for a minute. I don't know if I think I did or not. I do actually feel at least semi-justified in fucking Holly. I don't know if I did or not. For argument's sake I say, "Sure."

She says, "Well, that doesn't sound too sincere. But you just need to go back to the Mrs. and say, 'Listen, honey, I fucked up.'"

I say, "I don't know if it's that simple."

And this is when the prostitute turns to me and says something I'll probably remember for the rest of my life. She says, "It's always that simple. *I fucked up. I'm sorry.* That's all she wants to hear—that you're sorry for fucking up, and that you've learned something from it, and that because of whatever you learned you're not even capable of doing it again. Everyone makes mistakes. She just wants to know that you know it was a mistake. Unless you kill somebody, it's pretty rare that the mistake is bad enough to fuck something up forever."

When I get back to my hotel room at the Marriott, I force myself to jerk off thinking about Alyna's ass and tits. Memories of fucking Holly creep in from time to time, but when I blow my load I'm thinking back to a time when Alyna sucked my dick in the shower of my old apartment a few months after we first started dating. I fucked up.

chapter forty-one

The Transfer

I haven't seen or talked to Holly since the party, and when I walk into the office Monday morning I'm not exactly sure what to expect. It doesn't seem out of the realm of possibility that she'll be sucking Lonnie's dick while she's getting fucked by some asshole from Legal or something similar. This is not the case, though.

I walk out of the elevator and onto our floor, and just as I do every morning, I pass Holly's desk on the way to my office. And, just like every morning, she's on Facebook and she says, "Hey," when I walk past. But in a divergence from my usual practice, this time I don't respond. I just go to my office, sit down, and open a spreadsheet. I don't look at her Facebook page. I don't send her an IM. I even try not to look at her, but that can't be helped. I take in a few long glances at her ass and her back and try as hard as I can to remember the good things about her. In some way they all involve fucking.

I go back over almost every second we spent together and I can't recall one in which I was having fun with her that my dick wasn't in her or I wasn't high or drunk. Even if this isn't true, I force myself to believe it is. I force myself to take the image of her I have in my head and transform it into that of a retarded person who's really good at fucking and nothing else. Then I get an IM from her. It reads, "Are we cool?"

I'm not sure how to respond to this. The fact that she's even asking this can only mean that there's still some possibility of fucking her again, and I can't discount this. I try to force myself to imagine the taste of some other guy's semen in her mouth, but I know rationally that she's probably brushed her teeth and possibly even used mouthwash. I'm not sure I'm capable of never fucking her again if I know I still have the opportunity. The same logic the Four Seasons prostitute gave me about my marriage can also be applied here. Holly just fucked up. Her IM is her way of saying she fucked up. My fingers are on the keyboard and I'm about to write her back. I'm about to tell her that we're cool, and to see if she wants to get dinner after work, which always leads to fucking in my hotel room.

Then I look out at her and see her flirting with one of the young guys from the mail room. He has his hands on her shoulders. They're laughing. I don't know if it's her age, or her looks, or a combination thereof, but with a girl like Holly this will always be the case. She has too many options and too little regard for the importance of intimacy to ever give anyone anything approaching normal. I imagine her at my age, after her tits have started sagging, after her ass isn't quite as perky, after guys stop paying her the same attention they do now, and I feel like I know what she'll be. She'll just be another pretty girl who wasted her youth thinking it would never end, or not even realizing what she had while she had it. It's kind of sad, but I take comfort in the fact that I had my dick in every one of her holes when she was in her prime.

I minimize my IM window and compose the following e-mail to the head of HR:

"Holly McDonnel has performed with skill at her position of unpaid intern in the Accounts department. Her assignments, however, have come to a conclusion, and I strongly recommend utilizing her talents in another department, possibly Legal. Thank you."

I send the e-mail, and by the end of the day someone from HR comes up and talks to her. Before she leaves our floor she comes into my office and says, "Hey. They're moving me to Legal."

I say, "Oh. Good luck."

She says, "What's up? Are you, like, still pissed off about the other night?"

I say, "No, Holly, I'm not mad at all. I get it. I get your whole thing and it's fine. It's just not something I'm interested in anymore."

She slumps down in the chair across from my desk and starts crying. I panic. I don't know if I should shut the door so that no one sees her crying in my office or if that would be even more conspicuous. Through tears she says, "I'm sorry. Please can we still hang out?"

I say, "No. I don't really think that's a good idea anymore," and then I realize: She's never been rejected before in her life. Every one of the hundreds of guys that comment on her status on Facebook have all either fucked her and want to again or are trying to for the first time. And that's the thing she needs. She needs to know that every guy she ever meets approves of her and wants her, and that's more important to her than having anything real with any one of them. I kind of feel bad for her. I kind of feel bad for her entire generation, because they all seem to be like that to me. I hope that, by the time my daughter is Holly's age, Facebook has become something else and girls have become something else. I briefly wonder what I'll be doing in twenty years, if I'll be fucking a girl who is my daughter's age.

I hand Holly a Kleenex and say, "We had fun. I think we just wanted different things out of this and that's fine."

She says, "What did you want? A girlfriend or something?"

The simple answer to that question would be yes, but I say, "I wanted a connection, I guess. You know, just to feel like you gave a shit about it."

She says, "But we have a connection. You bought me a MacBook."

I say, "No, we don't. I don't think we ever really did."

She sucks up her tears and says, "Okay. Bye, I guess."

I say, "Bye," and she walks out of my office.

Getting Legal

Before my lunch break, I Google "marijuana doctors" and find one a few miles from the office. Dr. Kenneth Ridgemont III. I call his office and a girl answers. I'm not sure what to say. I say, "Hi, I was wondering, do I need to make an appointment, or how exactly does this work?"

The girl says, "No appointment necessary. Just come in anytime you want. The examination will take about fifteen minutes."

I say, "Okay, thanks."

I head over to a nondescript two-story office building on my lunch break and make my way to suite 206, which has no placard outside indicating that it's a doctor's office, just a plain door marked 206. There is no doorbell, so I knock and hear the same girl's voice that answered the phone. She says, "Door's open."

I walk into a small room about the size of my own office. The girl I talked to sits behind a desk. She's pretty clearly high out of her mind. She says, "Hi," then hands me a clipboard with one sheet of paper attached to it and says, "Fill this out and the doctor will see you shortly."

The form asks for my name, driver's-license number, phone

number—no address—and my symptoms. I have no idea what to
write, but I figure I'll have to make whatever symptoms I list believ-
able; I might even have to do a little acting. I write "back pain" and
"insomnia." These shouldn't be too hard to fake.

I give the form back to the girl behind the desk and she says,
"Great. The doctor is ready for you now."

A door behind her desk opens and out steps a guy wearing jeans
and a T-shirt under a doctor's white coat. He says, "Hello. Please follow
me to the examination room," like he's a robot. I'm assuming he's following some carefully scripted protocol, quite possibly a routine that's
required by law for this man to maintain whatever barely legal medical
license he has. I follow him into the so-called examination room, half-
thinking I'm going to get clubbed in the fucking head and wake up in
a gutter with my wallet missing.

I sit down in a regular chair in the examination room. There is no
examination table. In fact, there are no items in the entire room giving
even the vague impression that this is a medical office at all. There are
a few shelves with office supplies, like toner and reams of paper, but no
cotton balls, no bottles of hydrogen peroxide or rubbing alcohol, no
charts of the human ear. The only thing remotely medical is a stetho-
scope hanging around the good doctor's neck. It looks like he got it out
of a doctor play-set from Toys R Us.

He reads over the form I filled out. I'm expecting him to ask me
questions, to verify that I am, in fact, in need of medicinal marijuana.
Instead he says, "Okay, everything looks good here. Now I'm going to
perform the physical examination," and I'm ready for the clubbing.

He bends down, takes one of my legs by the ankle, and extends it
outward until my leg is straight. He says, "Great," and puts my leg back
down on the ground. He then puts two fingers on my sternum, gently
taps it, and says, "Perfect." Then he says, "Turn your head please."
Here comes the clubbing. I turn my head and he puts the fake stetho-
scope on my Adam's apple and says, "Exactly."

Then the doctor whips out the form I filled out, signs his name on it, and says, "I'm going to prescribe you medicinal cannabis. Cannabis is most effective and least harmful to your body if ingested in the form of an edible, or if inhaled after being vaporized. Please take this to my receptionist and you're all set."

The doctor leaves the room. I hand the form to the receptionist. She charges me forty dollars and I walk out with a signed and notarized document that allows me to purchase marijuana legally at one of hundreds of stores that sell it in Los Angeles.

chapter forty-two

Mea Culpa

I call Alyna. She says, "Do you have those papers signed?"

I say, "No."

She says, "Well fucking sign them, please, so we can just get this all over with."

I say, "Can we get dinner or something? I want to just talk about things before we actually go through with this."

She says, "We tried that. Remember?"

I say, "I know. But it's different now."

She says, "You're fucking right it's different now. I want a divorce now."

I say, "I'm sorry. I just want you to know that I'm sorry for all of this."

She says, "Great. Sign the papers," and hangs up on me. I realize this is going to take a much stronger approach than I had initially anticipated, so I get in my car and drive from the Marriott to the house, to my house, to our house.

I ring the doorbell and Alyna answers. She's surprised. She says, "Now's not a real good time."

I say, "Why? Do you have company?"

She says, "Yes."

I say, "Who?"

My question is answered by the company in question when I hear the lawyer I went to see, who claimed to be the biggest fucking shark in the ocean, say from my own fucking living room, "Alyna, I don't actually recommend talking to your spouse right now, from a legal standpoint."

I push past Alyna and walk in to see this motherfucker sitting in my living room. I say, "I met with you. How can you be my wife's attorney, too?"

He says, "No law against it. And you didn't hire me anyway, remember? So . . . sorry, pal, you got the biggest shark sitting on your couch. Soon to be your wife's couch."

I say, "Get out."

He says, "Alyna, do you want me to leave?"

I say, "This is legally my fucking house. Get out."

He says, "Understood," and tries to give me his card as he moves to the door. Before he leaves, he looks at Alyna and says, "Get him out of here as soon as you can."

Once he's gone I say, "Are you and him . . . ?"

She rolls her eyes and says, "Be fucking serious."

I notice Andy and Jane are gone. I say, "Where are the kids?"

She says, "Isabelle took them for a few hours so I could meet with my lawyer."

I say, "That guy is such a sleazy piece of shit. I can't believe you picked him."

She says, "He was pretty highly recommended by one of my . . . Look, what the hell are you doing here?"

I sit down on the couch and say, "I don't know how else to say what I need to say except that I'm sorry, Alyna. I'm sorry for everything I've put you through, for everything I've put the kids through, and it's over. And I want to do the right thing."

She says, "You know, there was a time when I was willing to forgive it all—in the very beginning. I was even willing to take some responsibility in it. But when I gave you the chance, you just—you didn't do anything. It was like you needed time to make a fucking decision about what was more valuable to you, our family or some twenty-year-old slut."

For a brief second I actually think about being honest with Alyna, with the mother of my children, with the woman I cheated on. I think about trying to explain to her what it's like to be a guy whose main sexual outlet is jerking off to porn every night after his wife falls asleep. I think about trying to explain to her what it's like to fuck a girl like Holly, a girl who is hotter and better at fucking than any girl I've ever met, including Alyna. I think about trying to explain to her that I had to fuck her, that I didn't want to end up like Todd's dad on his deathbed wondering what it might have been like. I think about trying to explain to her that, even if she forgives me and I move back in, I'll still be thinking about fucking every other girl I see. And I think about telling her that I might even cheat on her again, because now that I know how incredible fucking someone else can be, I honestly don't know if I'll be able to stop myself if the opportunity arises. I think about trying to explain what it's like to be a man in his mid-thirties who is married to a woman who has clearly lost interest in fucking him. I say, "It will never happen again. I love our family. I love you and I just wanted to come over here tonight to have the chance to tell you that in person. I want to make this right. I want us to be okay again, if we can be."

She says, "*Were* we okay, though? I mean, why did this happen in the first place?"

I say, "We were okay. I just fucked up. People fuck up. And I really am sorry."

She says, "We weren't okay. And I feel like the problems we had could have been fixed with time. But now . . . how can I even think about any of that sex stuff Roland was talking about before? If our problems had us teetering on the edge of a cliff before, all of this seems like it might have pushed us over the edge, you know?"

I say, "I think we can do this. And I think that, if we don't at least give it a try, at least really make an effort to repair this, we'll always wonder if we should have." This gets to her. This makes sense to her. I say, "I know now that what I did was terrible, and I've learned from it. I really have."

She says, "What did you learn?"

I realize I was just saying words I thought she wanted to hear. I didn't know she was going to quiz me on it so quickly. But I still manage to conjure up a response: "I've learned what's most important to me—you and the kids. Us. This life we've built is the most important thing that I'll ever know, and I can't just let it slip away. I think, I hope, that you can't either."

We talk for another hour or so. The conversation involves a lot of me apologizing and trying to remind Alyna of the good times we had before I cheated on her. She seems receptive, or at least that's what I infer from the fact that she's allowing me to stay and talk. She keeps repeating "I don't know" after most of my attempts at apology or reconciliation. I attempt to appeal to her sense of duty as a mother by mentioning that I don't want the kids to have to go through life without a father, a real father, around. This seems to get the best reaction out of her, or at least the closest reaction to forgiveness that I can detect. I hope that she'll come sit next to me on the couch, but she never does. She just stands by the kitchen counter, leaning against it, sometimes picking up her car keys and mindlessly staring at them as I talk. Occasionally she'll offer something like, "Even if we work this out, things are going to be different—a lot different. Will you be able to handle that? I'm talking about the stuff we talked about at dinner that night." I assure her that I'm willing to accept all the old demands and any she might want to add to the list.

Throughout the conversation, I take a quick survey of the living room and see that my Xbox is still plugged into the TV. All of my

DVDs and Xbox games are still on the shelf where I kept them. My laptop computer is still sitting on the counter in the kitchen. She never put any of my shit in storage. That must have been a bluff, a move designed to put pressure on me to get rid of Holly. This gives me hope that she never really wanted a divorce in the first place. Near the end of the conversation I say, "I don't know what it would take, but I'm willing to do anything to go back to the way things were."

I think this gets her legitimately teetering. I look over on the coffee table and see a picture of our entire family. We took it at Disneyland about six months ago. I fucking hate Disneyland. It's even worse when you're pushing a kid around in a stroller while the other one is sprinting around demanding to ride the fucking teacups two hundred times. That picture reminds me of nothing but one of the most miserable days of my life, but it's that picture, that image of me holding Jane, who unbeknownst to me had a diaper full of shit at the time, and Andy screaming in a pair of Mickey Mouse ears, and Alyna doing her best fake smile, that breaks me down and I start tearing up.

Maybe it was because I was too busy fucking Holly, or because I didn't really know how I wanted it all to resolve, but I've never cried through any of this. The real emotional weight of the situation never set in, but sitting there on my couch trying to imagine any scenario in which I am not a father to my children and even, on some level, a husband to Alyna makes my eyes sting and my nasal passages swell a little. Alyna sees what's going on as I wipe one of my eyes. She says, "Look. I appreciate you coming over here and saying all of this. I really do. But I don't think anything's getting figured out tonight. I have to go get the kids. Why don't you go back to your hotel? Give me some time to think."

To some degree I feel like I know how she must have felt when she laid out her demands and wanted an immediate reaction from me that I couldn't give her. In that moment, I want her to take me back. I want to see my kids tonight. I want to sleep in my own bed again. But I understand. I say, "Okay."

She walks me to the door and I don't try for a hug. She doesn't offer one, either. I say, "Tell the kids I love them. And I guess I'll wait to hear from you."

She nods. I turn to leave and she says, "Tomorrow."

I turn around, expecting her to say that she'll have some decision on this by tomorrow, but she says, "Tomorrow night I have a parent-teacher evaluation at Andy's school. Why don't you come?"

I say, "Okay. I'll be there."

In my hotel room I watch *American Idol* and think to myself that Alyna is probably doing the same thing in our living room with Andy and Jane. Before I go to sleep that night, I notice, for the first time since I started fucking Holly, that the gnawing in the pit of my stomach is gone. When I was fucking Holly and Alyna didn't know, I was constantly worried she'd find out. When I was fucking her and Alyna did know, I was constantly worried that I'd never see my kids again. I close my eyes, and the last thought that goes through my mind before I sleep is a memory of how Jane's head smelled once when she was lying on my chest and I was watching football in my living room.

chapter forty-three

Evaluation

I meet Alyna in the parking lot of Andy's school. She says, "Thanks
for coming."

I say, "There's no way I would have missed this."

She says, "I know, but still, thanks." The way she says this makes
me think that Andy's teacher has become aware of our separation
somehow, that I'm walking into what will amount to a two-woman tag-
team kickfest of my ball bag. I hope this is not the case as Alyna and I
head into Andy's school without touching one another.

Once inside, we head to Andy's classroom, where Mrs. Banks is
waiting for us. She shakes our hands and goes through all the bullshit
protocol that's probably mandated by the school board or maybe even
the state. She sits us down, opens a little book with some notes in it,
and says, "First of all, I'd like to let you know that Andy is certainly one
of the brightest kids in the class."

I say, "That's great."

Mrs. Banks says, "Yes, it is. He excels at understanding any concept that I present in class, in a wide range of subjects, and he seems

to have a proclivity for the visual arts as well as for music. Twice a week we let the kids get out instruments and form their own bands and put on shows for one another. Andy particularly enjoys this, and he's taken a liking to the drums. My apologies if he starts requesting a drum set for his next birthday," then laughs a weird, forced laugh. Alyna smiles. I just keep looking at Mrs. Banks and say, "So this is all great news."

Mrs. Banks closes her notebook and says, "That is all great news. But there was one thing I wanted to speak to you about." Then she stands up and says, "If you'll follow me over to the art wall, I'd like to show you Andy's latest creation."

We walk over to a wall covered with maybe fifteen or twenty drawings done by four-year-olds. A few of them aren't bad, but most are shit. Most are just scribbles. Some have barely recognizable impressions of human faces. I zero in on one, though. It's a skeleton getting shot by a guy with a machine gun. I say, "Wow, this one is really good."

Mrs. Banks says, "Yes, that's Andy's."

Alyna is impressed by it, too. She says, "Wow. I don't want to insult the other kids but it's pretty clearly better than the others by, like, a lot."

Mrs. Banks says, "Yes. He's quite talented. He clearly exhibits the ability to create an image that is very representative of the idea he is trying to convey. But it's the meaning behind the image that concerns me a little bit."

I say, "What was the assignment?"

Mrs. Banks says, "It was to draw something that you think represents happiness."

Alyna says, "Oh my god."

Mrs. Banks says, "Yes. Some of Andy's artwork, this most recent piece included, suggests a level of distress that I think we might want to address in this evaluation."

Alyna says, "Is he not getting along with the other kids?"

Mrs. Banks says, "No, it's nothing like that. He gets along with everyone very well. He's actually very socially gifted, in addition to his other talents. All the other kids seem to enjoy his company very much."

I say, "Then what's the deal here?"

Mrs. Banks says, "At this stage, these drawings aren't really anything to be overly alarmed with. Children will quite often create violent or frightening imagery in an assignment like this if they feel the need to convey to an adult that they're not feeling all that happy lately. Which is what I wanted to speak to you about. Is everything okay at home?"

As she asks this question, I'm reminded of a bunch of shitty movies in which a teacher or someone outside the immediate family asks this question with the overt implication that the kid is being abused. The conversation must have conjured the same type of reaction for Alyna, because she beats me to the punch. "Are you asking us if Andy's getting abused at home?"

Mrs. Banks says, "Oh no. No, no, no. I didn't mean to imply that. It's very clear that this isn't the case at all. Without prying, I'm just curious if everything is stable at home, or if there have been any significant changes in your relationship or your behavior. Maybe due to a situation at work, or anything at all. At this age children begin to learn how to read emotion in their parents, and quite often that can reflect in their own emotional well-being."

It's clear to me that Mrs. Banks doesn't know shit about the fact that I haven't lived at home for a while, or about me fucking Holly, or about any of it. I don't know how to respond to the question. I don't want to air our dirty laundry, but some piece of me thinks that Alyna might appreciate it if I own up and say I've been a shitty husband recently but I'm working on it. I'm a second away from opening my mouth to that end when Alyna looks at me and says, "Well, you have been working a lot more lately, and coming home late, and Andy isn't seeing as much of you as he usually does." Then she turns to Mrs. Banks and says, "Could that be it?"

Mrs. Banks says, "That could absolutely be it. And, again, this isn't any cause for real alarm unless it persists or becomes worse."

I say, "How would it become worse?"

Mrs. Banks says, "Well, if his feelings were to manifest through actions instead of his artwork, that could be problematic."

I say, "I see. Well, I, uh, don't really know what the situation with my job is going to be like. It's not really up to me." I look at Alyna and say, "It's actually completely out of my hands."

Alyna looks at me and says, "It seems to me like you can probably figure something out so you can spend some more time at home this week."

I look at her and say, "You think so?"

Alyna says, "It seems pretty likely."

Mrs. Banks says, "I'm sorry, I was under the impression that you were a stay-at-home mother. Do you two work together now?"

Alyna says, "I am. We don't work together. I was just saying, for Andy's sake, I'm sure we can figure it out."

In that moment, for the first time in all of this I start to feel normal again. It's not happiness. It's not relief. It doesn't feel good. It just feels normal.

Getting Old

I've had ingrown hairs before. This one is particularly painful and it's a fucking pubic hair. Thankfully it's not on the base of my dick, but more in the general pubic area, kind of toward my left hip. It's formed a whitehead, and I figure I should pop it, get the shit out and let it heal, so it stops causing me pain as soon as possible.

In the bathroom I pull my pants down, kind of squat over the toilet for some reason, and bend over so I can get my eyes as close to the area as I can. I'm sure I look like some hunchbacked psychopath who's on the verge of jerking off, but it must be done.

I get a thumbnail on either side of the offender and give it a good squeeze. It pops, and a little pus comes out, along with about half an inch of curly pubic hair. At this point, two things happen: I'm happy to have the hair free, and I'm horrified to see that the hair is, to my knowledge, the first gray hair anywhere on my body.

chapter forty-four

Welcome Home

I jerk off one last time in my bed at the Marriott, thinking about all the times I fucked Holly in it. I treat it as a kind of symbolic last hurrah with her, even though I know I'm going to think about her asshole and her tits and how she sucked dick every time I jerk off for the foreseeable future, and I assume I will be doing a lot of jerking off until Alyna actually lets me fuck her again, if she does. She added a demand to her list that I get an STD test, which conjures two reactions in me. I'm slightly scared that it might come back with something, because I did fuck Holly a few times without a rubber, but I'm also encouraged that Alyna would ask for this, because it means she's already thought about fucking me again.

I blow my load in the sheets and leave it there for the housekeepers to clean up. I take a final shit and give the place one last look, trying to force myself to see it as a bad place, a place I should have never had to be in at all, but the memories of fucking Holly are too good for me to do that. I know I'll always think fondly of this hotel. Every time I drive by, whether Alyna and the kids are in the car with me or not,

I'll always remember it as something special. I got to fuck my Maria Reynaldi, and I got to do it here in this room.

I toss the room key on the bed and walk out.

When I get home, even though all I have with me is my duffel bag, it still feels like I'm moving back in. The kids are happy to see me. Andy gives me a big hug and says, "Are you finally done with work now, Daddy?"

I say, "Yep. All done."

He says, "Finally. Jesus Christ."

I look at Alyna. She says, "He just started saying it a few days ago." I laugh and he says it again. She says, "Don't laugh or he'll just keep doing it."

I say, "But it's funny."

Andy says, "You think I'm funny, Daddy?"

I say, "I think you're extremely funny," and tickle him until he screams and I feel more normal than I did at the parent-teacher evaluation.

I pick up Jane and she says, "Daddy. Drink."

Alyna hands me a cup of juice from the counter and I help Jane take a sip. She says, "Thanks you," and I feel even more normal. These small things are not Holly. These small things are not fucking. These small things are not exciting. These small things are my life, and the realization of this fact makes me neither happy nor sad. It just makes me feel normal, and that is better than not feeling normal.

We let the kids stay up a little later than they normally would, and I watch *American Idol* with my family, and we eat a pizza from Papa John's. We drink soda and we laugh. When the show is over, Alyna gives the kids their bath and I play *Modern Warfare*. When the kids are clean and in bed, Alyna comes out into the living room and says, "I'm going to bed."

I say, "Okay."

She says, "I know this is weird, but are you coming?"

I say, "If you want me to."

She says, "What else are you going to do? Sleep on the couch?"

I say, "I'm going to do whatever makes you comfortable."

She says, "We're going to have to sleep in the same bed at some point. Might as well get it out of the way."

In bed we do not fuck. We do nothing that even approaches fucking. I don't expect us to. I also don't expect Alyna to do what she does. For several minutes I lie staring at the ceiling, comparing the pattern of the flecked white surface with the ceiling in the hotel room. Alyna is on her side of the bed with her back to me. I think about the last time Holly and I were in the same bed. After we fucked she rolled over to the edge of the bed, like Alyna is now, and I stared at the ceiling, like I'm doing now.

Just as I'm trying not to think about the fact that the only difference between Alyna and Holly in this circumstance is that Holly fucked the living shit out of me before rolling over and offering me no affection, Alyna rolls over to face me and without saying anything snuggles into my armpit and puts a hand on my chest.

I'm frozen by it. I don't know if she's trying to initiate a reconciliation fuck or if she's just trying to get used to sleeping with me in the bed again. Eventually she says, "We have to do this, right? And I'm not talking about sex. Don't get the wrong idea. But is this okay? I mean, is this weird?"

I lower one of my arms and put it around her as I say, "No, this isn't weird at all. I think it's completely normal."

I feel her out-of-shape body against my out-of-shape body and it feels completely normal as I drift into a dreamless sleep with my children and my wife sleeping under the same roof that I am.

chapter forty-five

Feels Like the First Time

I've been home for a week and a half when my STD test comes back clean. I breathe a small sigh of relief that none of the possible nightmare scenarios I concocted in my head are true. Aside from the obvious and almost impossible scenario in which I got AIDS or something, I did have a minor concern that I might have gotten herpes, in which case Alyna would definitely have made me fuck with a rubber for the rest of my life, or just never fucked me at all, or possibly even divorced me. But I'm clean.

After work I show her the test results and she says, "That's good news, I guess."

I say, "What do you mean, you guess?"

She says, "Nothing. I mean it's good news."

That night, I decide to try to initiate our first fuck with me back in the house. I help her bathe the kids and put them to bed, and then, based on the level of comfort she's developed with me when we cuddle at night in bed, I assume she'll be receptive to an impromptu back rub. At first she's clearly hesitant to relax with my hands on her, but then she gives in a little bit and says, "Fuck, I needed this."

I keep rubbing for ten or fifteen minutes, and then I decide to make my move by kissing the back of her neck. She immediately moves away from me and says, "What the fuck are you doing?"

I say, "Kissing my wife's neck."

She says, "Whoa. Back rub is one thing, but this is another thing."

I say, "I'm not trying to push anything. I just thought maybe tonight would be the night, you know?"

She says, "I know we're eventually going to have to do this—"

I want to dive through a window. That phrase, "have to do this," makes it clear to me that she has even less interest in me sexually than she did before I cheated on her, which was almost zero. Where before she might have found sex with me to be a boring chore she needed to do every once in a while, clearly she now finds it a deplorable event she's going to have to endure against her will. I think about scrapping the whole idea. I think about just telling Alyna that it was all a mistake trying to make this work, and then walking out.

I ask myself why it was so important to make this work, to salvage my relationship with a woman who will very likely never want to fuck me like she used to. My kids are certainly one of the main reasons, but there's something beyond the obvious reason. From somewhere deep down, another feeling emerges—that I actually miss my old life, my married life. I miss sitting in a chair watching football with my daughter asleep on my chest. I miss having full cable and a backyard. I miss sleeping in a bed that's not in a hotel or a dorm room. I miss being an adult.

I say, "We don't *have* to do anything. I want you to be comfortable with this. I want you to be happy that I'm back."

She says, "I am happy you're back. You know that. I want our kids to have their father back."

I say, "What about you?"

She says, "What about me?"

I say, "Do you want your husband back?"

She says, "Do you want me to be honest?"

There is no way whatever she says next will be anything I actually want to hear. I say, "Of course."

She says, "You're still the same dad Jane and Andy's always had. They don't know what you did. They don't know anything except that you had to 'work late' for a little while. And I want it that way. Believe me, I don't want them to ever know what happened. I want you to be their dad forever and not the shitbag dad who cheated on their mom."

I say, "Thanks."

She says, "But to me, you're not the same husband. The husband I married is gone. I honestly don't think I can ever think of you as that same person again."

This is what I imagine it feels like to hear that you've been diagnosed with lung or brain cancer. There is no hope for something better. Each successive moment you live will be slightly worse than the last, until you die.

I say, "So what do we do, then?"

She says, "I don't know."

We brush our teeth next to each other in silence. We get in bed next to each other in silence. She doesn't snuggle up next to me like she's been doing. Eventually she says, "There aren't any condoms anyway."

This is my opening. I say, "I got a vasectomy. Remember?"

She says, "Really?"

I say, "Yeah. You were the one who wanted me to do it. It was scheduled and everything, so I decided I should still do it."

She says, "Why?"

And I feel like da Vinci painting the final brushstroke on the *Mona Lisa* as I say, "Because it was a decision we made together and I always had hope that we'd be in the same bed again, in the same house. That this would work out."

She moves toward me and kisses me. She's nervous. I try to go down on her but she says, "No, let's just do this." She only touches my dick once, when she climbs on top of me and positions it so it's angled toward the opening of her pussy, which is not wet at all. She sits back on my dick a few times, inching the head in little by little as it sticks to the sides of her dry vagina.

I say, "Just let me go down on you."

She says, "No. Just . . . it's almost in."

She sits down on my dick a few more times with more force. I'm starting to lose my boner as I think about how devoid of any sexual enthusiasm this whole thing is. Then she finally gets my dick in her and nature takes over.

I thrust upward from the bottom into her pussy as she sits motionless on top of me. She looks down at me with what looks like contempt on her face. The last memory I have of fucking her is similar. I only have to replace the look of contempt with boredom. I say, "We really don't have to do this if you're not ready."

She says, "I'm never going to be ready. This will get better, but I just need to do this again with you or this might never feel right again."

I say, "Do you want me to do something different or another position or something?"

She says, "Just cum."

I say, "As fast as I can? Do you just want it over with?"

She starts crying and she says, "No. I need to know that you still want me like this, after you've been with that girl who's so much prettier than I am and so much younger and I'm sure so much better at sex."

I'm horrified. This is easily the worst sexual experience of my life. I can feel my dick shrinking. Eventually Alyna clinches her vagina and my limp dick pops out. She slumps down next to me and says, "I'm sorry."

I say, "No. There's nothing to be sorry for. I'm sorry. I'm the one who fucked this all up."

I hold my wife as she cries and I know that Roland was the tip of the fucking iceberg. I'm going to be in couples therapy for the rest of my life. As she sobs in my arms, I go through the possible scenarios in which I could turn this night around and still fuck her. They all involve some worldwide-destruction-type disaster that would give us only minutes to live. And even then I assume she'd probably rather spend her last minutes on Earth with the kids.

The sobbing eventually stops as she falls asleep and breathes heavily through her nose on my forearm, which is wet from her tears and snot. I can't sleep after having my dick in a pussy without blowing a load, so I sneak into my office and jerk off to some Brooke Lee Adams porn while my wife sleeps in a puddle of her own tears that I caused by fucking a twenty-one-year-old girl.

The Day Is Ruined

I still feel happy when I wake up in my own house. I wonder how long it will be before the old malaise sets in again, before the simple feeling of comfort in my own bed will be replaced by a dull boredom with every aspect of my life.

Alyna's not in bed with me, even though it's a Saturday. I can hear her out in the living room with the kids, watching what I think is *Dora the Explorer* based on the Spanish dialogue I can make out. I roll out of bed and head to the bathroom.

I turn the shower on, a little hotter than I normally do so I get that good sting that's just on the verge of pain, and I stand under the water for a minute letting it pound the back of my neck, breathing in the steam. I scrub down, wash my hair, use some of Alyna's conditioner, and then stand under the water for another minute once I'm rinsed off, just feeling the heat. I step out of the shower, dry off, brush my teeth, and shave. I feel clean. Then it hits me. I have to take a shit.

I'm disappointed, to say the least, as I sit down on the toilet. It was a great fucking shower. All I can hope is that my turd will be rock-hard—the kind that comes out so solid you probably wouldn't even have to wipe if you didn't want to. The turd I shit out isn't that type of turd. It's a fucking mashed banana. It takes seven wipes before the toilet paper comes back with only minor brown smudges instead of inch-thick pudding smears. It takes three more wipes after that to get to toilet paper with nothing on it. It doesn't matter, though. I feel dirty. The shower was wasted. I think about taking another one, but I decide not to. Instead I go into the bedroom, get dressed, and walk out into the living room hating the fact that I didn't even get to have a few hours of being completely clean after one of the best showers in recent memory. It's all fucking ruined.

chapter forty-six

Long Story Short

In the week after our first attempt to fuck, Alyna and I made no other attempts. She offered no blowjobs, no hand jobs, nothing even remotely sexual, although she would still cuddle with me in bed before sleep.

In the month after our first attempt at reconciliation sex, Alyna and I fucked once. It wasn't as terrible as the first attempt, but it wasn't good. She insisted we fuck doggy-style. I don't know if she thought that's what I wanted or if she just didn't want to look at my face. I came, but she didn't, and she refused my offer to go down on her to completion after we fucked.

In the six-month period after our first attempt at sex, we fucked five times, each time getting successively closer to the sexual relationship we had before I fucked Holly. In the last of these encounters, Alyna faked an orgasm. I thought about bringing it up to her, and using the argument that we have to be honest about everything in our relationship if it's going to work again, but I didn't. Instead I just accepted that this will very likely be the nature of our sexual relationship for the rest of our marriage.

In the year after our first attempt, we've fucked eighteen times. Each time, Alyna has insisted on fucking either doggy-style or with her on top. The sex is bad, and despite its unbearably low frequency it has become boring. The most recent sexual encounter we had ended with me pulling out and jerking off all over her back, in an effort to elicit some kind of a reaction from her when a new act was introduced without her prior approval. She didn't appear to notice and seemed as glad to have my dick out of her as she has seemed every time we've fucked.

We've been to three different marriage counselors, who all have said essentially the same thing where sex is concerned: that Alyna needs time, and no one can tell how much time it will take, because these situations are all unique, and the best thing I can do is give her that time without putting any pressure on her. Because I sought sexual gratification outside the relationship, I'm in no position to argue the point.

I have had no contact with Holly since the day I had her transferred to Legal. With time, she has become a fond memory for me. The things I found unattractive about her personality have dissipated, and I think about the various times we fucked when I masturbate, which is less and less frequently given my growing apathy toward sex of any kind, due to the nature of my sexual relationship with Alyna.

I see no hope that things will improve in the future. It will never be like it was. It will never be better than this.

chapter forty-seven

The End

There are twenty to thirty parents wandering around our backyard watching their kids fuck with my grill, some flowers Alyna planted last month, and a bird feeder that's been hanging from a tree since we bought the place. The parents do nothing about it. I recognize some of the parents from other kids' birthday parties, but I don't know any of their names.

It's strange to think about this pool of money that basically just gets pushed around for all of our kids' birthdays. Today Andy gets the full benefit. Next month it'll be one of these other little shitheads, and Andy will be tearing apart that shithead's dad's grill.

I'm drunk from what I think is my fifth Blue Moon when some dad comes up to me and says, "Nice party."

I don't care what he's saying and neither does he. We're just going through the protocol. I say, "Thanks."

He says, "They sure grow up fast, don't they?"

I say, "Yeah. They sure do."

We both take a swig of beer, he pats me on the back and says, "See ya 'round." This exact same conversation happens four or five more times with similar dead-eyed fathers who have given up hope for happiness but who experience no real sadness or discomfort in their lives either. They exist in a mediocre haze, content to serve out the remainder of their lives on the planet attending events like this, fucking their wives without meaning or enthusiasm when it's allowed, performing a job that has no real impact in the world and has no meaning to them personally, just as I do.

I try to remember what it was like to fuck Holly, what it was like to be excited about something. The memory is too far out, though. The entire experience has drifted into something so far removed from my actual life that is seems like it might not have happened at all. I still think about her from time to time and wonder what she might be doing. She's graduated by now. Maybe she's still sucking dick for weed. Maybe she's learned how to be affectionate. Maybe she even has a boyfriend.

After the party that night, as I tuck my son in, he says, "Daddy, did you have fun at the party today?"

I say, "Yeah, bud, I did. Did you?"

He says, "It was awesome. How many birthdays do I get to have?"

I say, "A bunch."

He says, "You've had more birthdays than me. Will they all be as fun as today?"

I want to tell him the truth. I want to tell my son that eventually birthdays become meaningless. You stop having parties, people stop giving you presents, and you stop caring that these things stop happening. I want to tell him that this doesn't just happen with birthdays. Eventually there's nothing that's fun in your life anymore. Eventually you come to understand that your life is just a series of similar meaningless days in which you try to find some sense of evenness and normalcy, and that becomes the best you can hope for.

Instead I kiss him on the head and I say, "They get even better."

He says, "I love you, Daddy."

I say, "I love you, too, bud." Then I turn off his light, get into bed with my wife, wait for her to fall asleep, and then sneak into the office, cue up some babysitter porn, and jerk off.